Fresh Everyday

OYING!

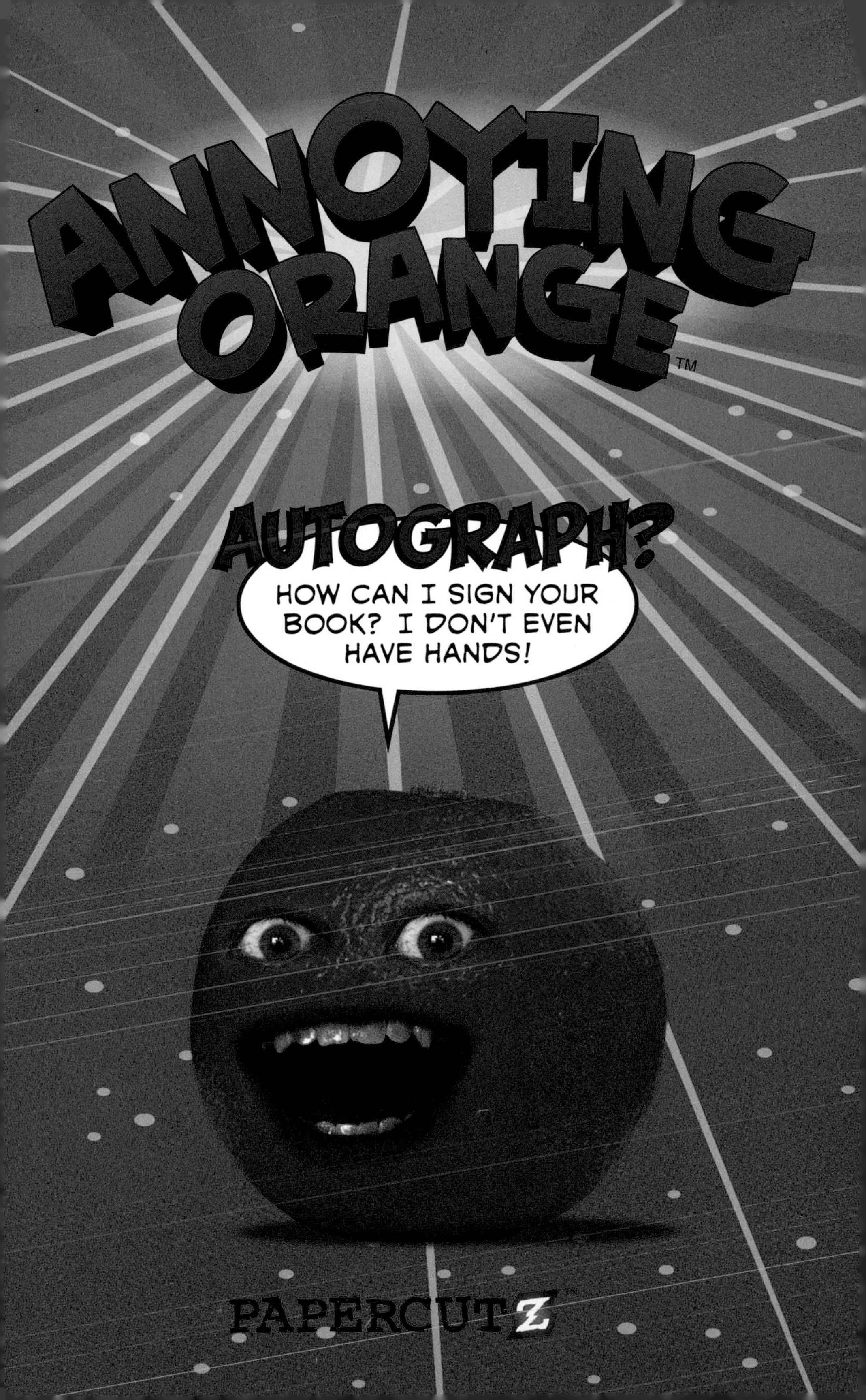
ANNOYING ORANGE™
AUTOGRAPH?
HOW CAN I SIGN YOUR BOOK? I DON'T EVEN HAVE HANDS!
PAPERCUTZ™

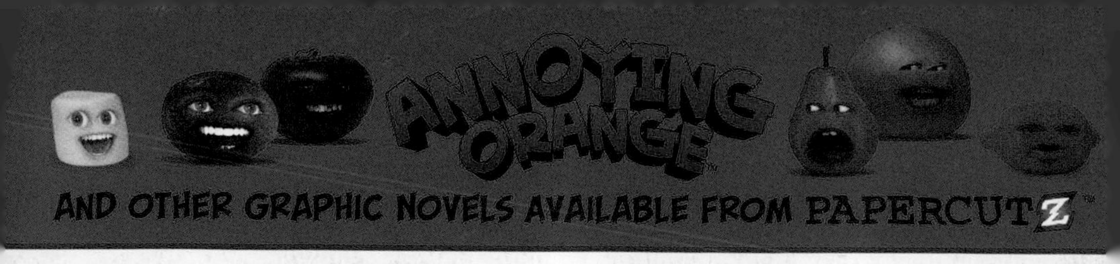
ANNOYING ORANGE
AND OTHER GRAPHIC NOVELS AVAILABLE FROM PAPERCUTZ

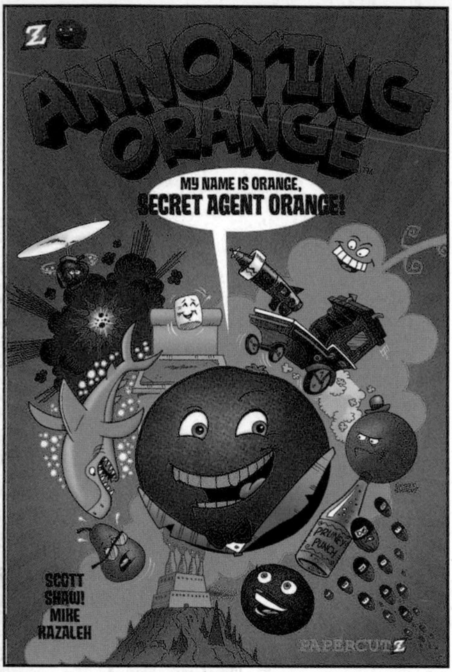
ANNOYING ORANGE
MY NAME IS ORANGE, SECRET AGENT ORANGE!
SCOTT SHAW! MIKE KAZALEH
PAPERCUTZ

ANNOYING ORANGE
Graphic Novel #1
"Secret Agent Orange"

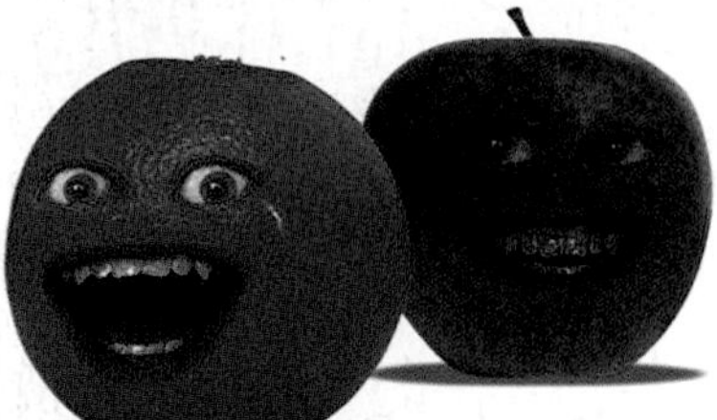

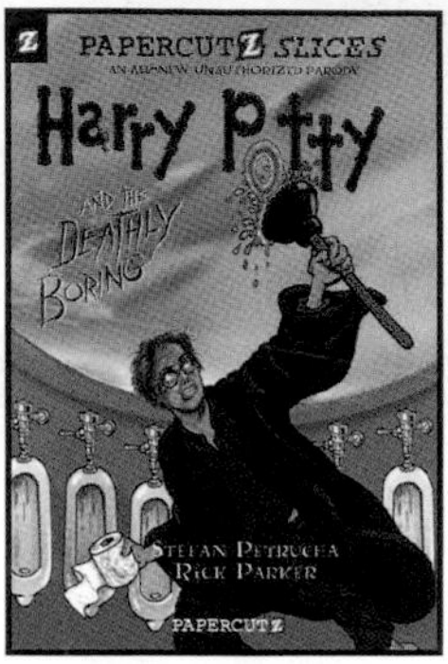
PAPERCUTZ SLICES
Harry Potty
AND THE DEATHLY BORING
STEFAN PETRUCHA
RICK PARKER
PAPERCUTZ

PAPERCUTZ SLICES
Graphic Novel #1
"Harry Potty and the Deathly Boring"

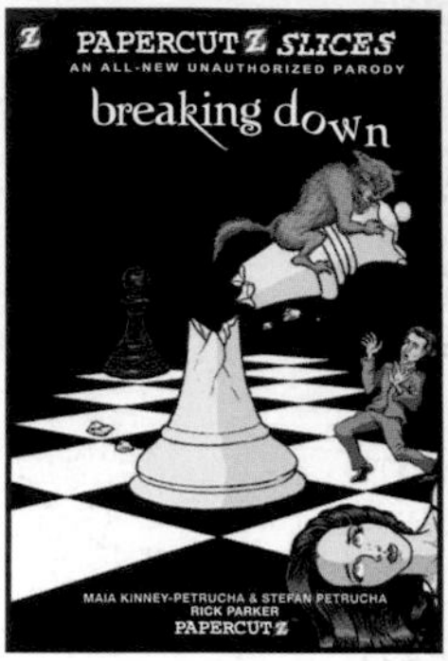
PAPERCUTZ SLICES
AN ALL-NEW UNAUTHORIZED PARODY
breaking down
MAIA KINNEY-PETRUCHA & STEFAN PETRUCHA
RICK PARKER
PAPERCUTZ

PAPERCUTZ SLICES
Graphic Novel #2
"breaking down"

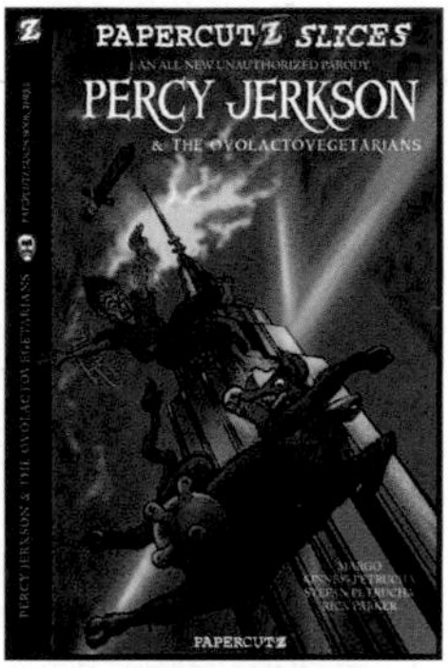
PAPERCUTZ SLICES
PERCY JERKSON
& THE OVOLACTOVEGETARIANS
PAPERCUTZ

PAPERCUTZ SLICES
Graphic Novel #3
"Percy Jerkson & The Ovolactovegetarians"

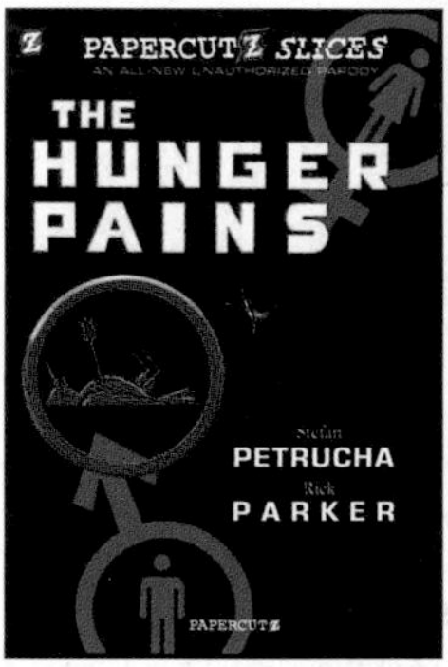
PAPERCUTZ SLICES
THE HUNGER PAINS
Stefan
PETRUCHA
Rick
PARKER
PAPERCUTZ

PAPERCUTZ SLICES
Graphic Novel #4
"The Hunger Pains"

ANNOYING ORANGE and PAPERCUTZ SLICES graphic novels, the print editions, are still available at booksellers everywhere.

Or order directly from Papercutz. ANNOYING ORANGE and PAPERCUTZ SLICES are available in paperback for $6.99 each; in hardcover for $10.99 each, please add $4.00 for postage and handling for the first book, and add $1.00 for each additional book. Make check payable to NBM Publishing.

Send to: Papercutz, 160 Broadway, Suite 700, East Wing, New York, NY 10038

Or call 800-886-1223 between 9-5 EST, M-F. Visa, MC, and AmEx accepted.

www.papercutz.com

ANNOYING ORANGE and PAPERCUTZ SLICES graphic novels are also available digitally wherever e-books are sold.

ANNOYING ORANGE

SECRET AGENT ORANGE

HEY! I'M A *GRAPHIC NOVEL!*

Annoying Orange is created by DANE BOEDIGHEIMER

MIKE KAZALEH – Writer & Artist

SCOTT SHAW! – Writer & Artist

LAURIE E. SMITH – Colorist

SCOTT SHAW! – Cover Artist

JAYJAY JACKSON – Cover Colorist

PAPERCUTZ
NEW YORK

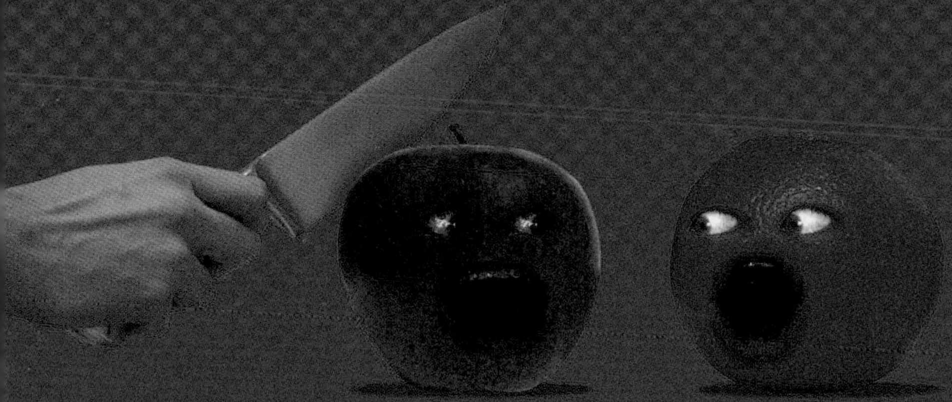

Annoying Orange

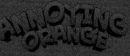

#1 "Secret Agent Orange"
"The Adventures of Marshmallow,"
"A Bedtime Story,"
"Bowling for Hollers,"
"Exciting Scenes from Our Next Graphic Novel,"
"Nerville, the Ladies' Man,"
"One Fine Day in the Produce Section,"
"Plum's Day Out,"
"The Salad Days of Grandpa Lemon,"
and "The Snow Contest"
Mike Kazaleh – Writer & Artist
Laurie E. Smith – Colorist
Tom Orzechowski – Letterer
"Grapefinger"
Scott Shaw! – Writer & Artist
Jayjay Jackson – Laurie E. Smith
Tom Orzechowski – Letterer
Janice Chiang – Letterer
Scott Shaw! – Cover Artist
Jayjay Jackson – Cover Colorist

Special thanks to: Gary Binkow, Tim Blankley, Dane Boedigheimer, Kristy Fagan, Spencer Grove, Teresa Harris, Reza Izad, Debra Joester, Polina Rey, Jess Richardson
Design & Production – Nelson Design Group, LLC
Director of Marketing – Jesse Post
Associate Editor – Michael Petranek
Jim Salicrup
Editor-in-Chief

ISBN: 978-1-59707-361-5 paperback edition
ISBN: 978-1-59707-362-2 hardcover edition

Printed in Canada
December 2012 by Friesens Printing
1 Printers Way
Altona, MB R0G 0B0

Distributed by Macmillan
First Printing

MEET THE FRUIT...

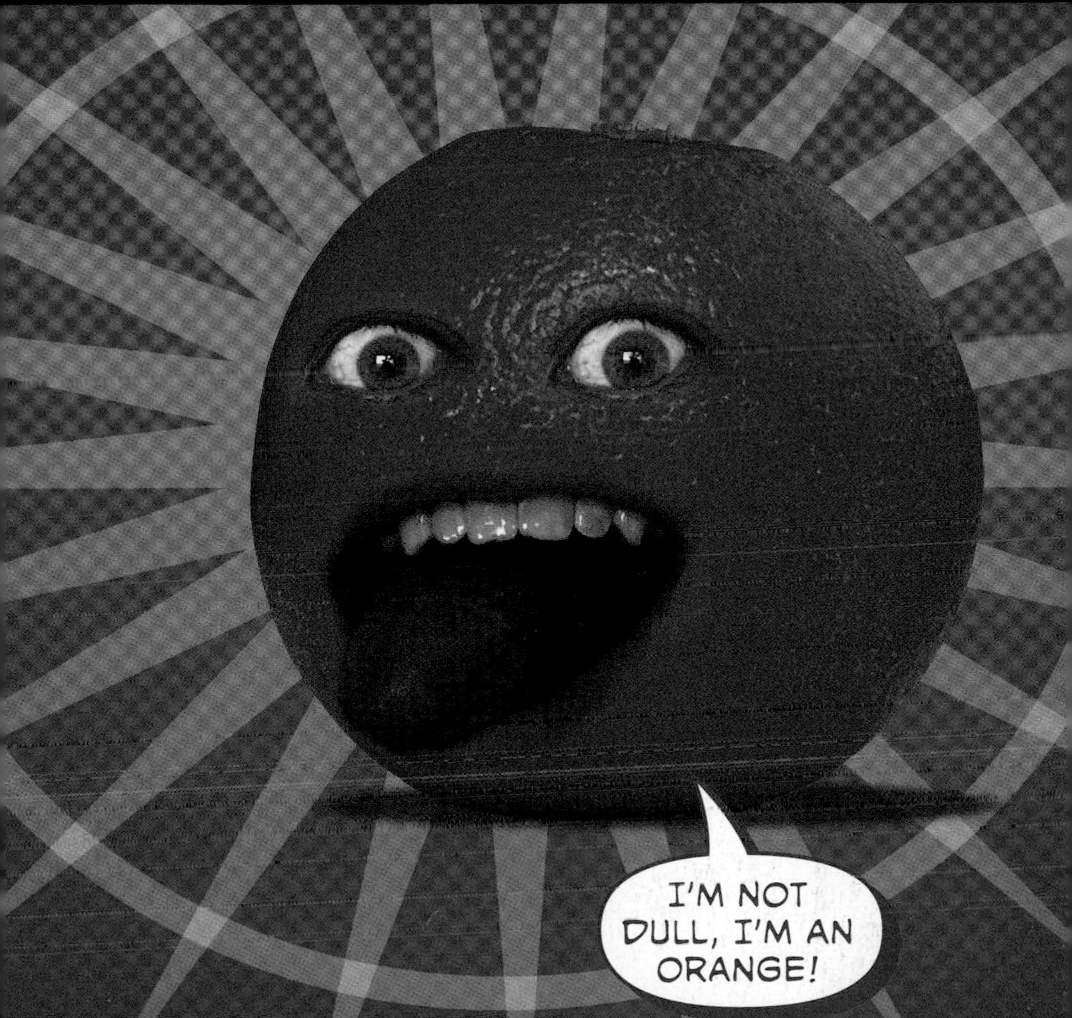
I'M NOT DULL, I'M AN ORANGE!

ORANGE

He's cute. He's sweet (sort of). He's Annoying. He's an Orange! To some, he's the king of comedy, the prince of puns, the earl of irritation! And to others, he's just a royal pun in the bottom. Call him what you will, but don't call him an apple. He hates that!

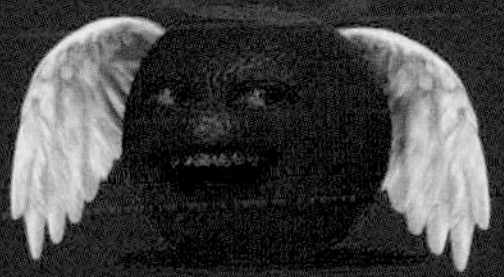

PEAR

Just like Orange, Pear is loaded with Vitamin C, but that's pretty much where similarities end. Despite their differences, Pear and Orange are best buds, a great "pair" of friends. Whenever Orange is around, Pear knows something interesting will happen.

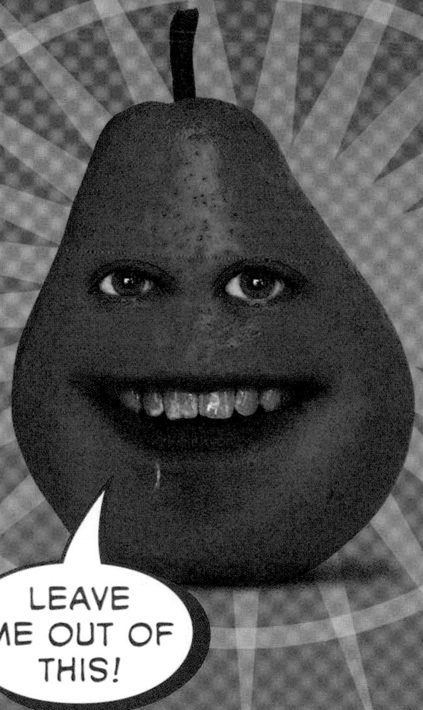
LEAVE ME OUT OF THIS!

MIDGET APPLE

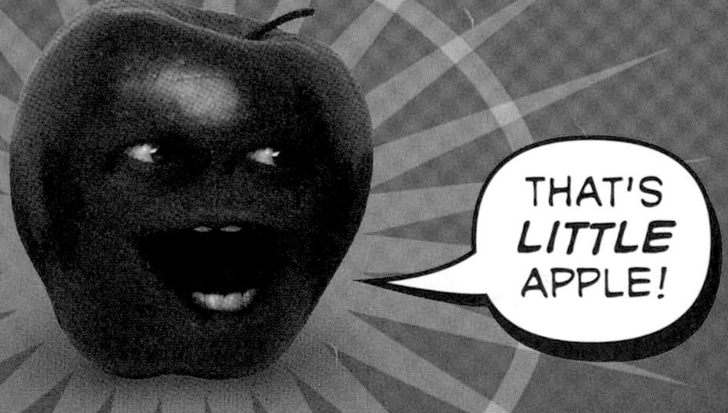
THAT'S *LITTLE* APPLE!

The only apple in Orange's entourage is Midget Apple. He constantly corrects others regarding his name, insisting that he's Little Apple (although Small and Tiny are also acceptable), but even he can't deny that he is indeed small. Midget Apple's best friend is Marshmallow. What Midget, er, ah, Little Apple lacks in size, he more than makes up for in laughs and loyalty.

PASSION FRUIT

Like the name implies, Passion Fruit is full of life! She's cheerful and calm, though she can get angry with Orange when he talks about others in an Annoying way. She's not just a hottie, but a smartie as well! Although she does have a little crush on Orange, and in turn she is the object of his affections! Too bad she doesn't know that!

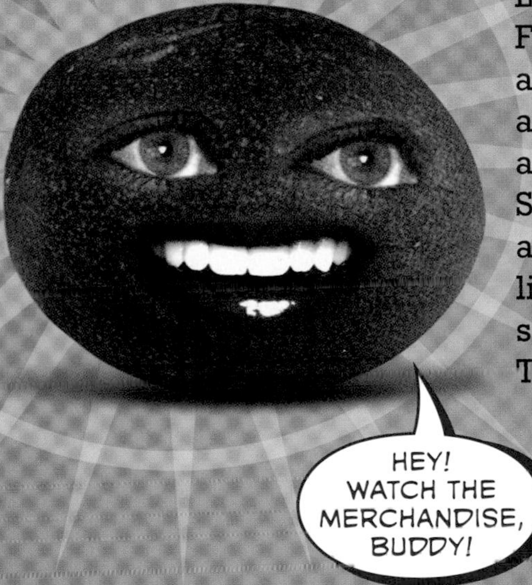
HEY! WATCH THE MERCHANDISE, BUDDY!

MARSHMALLOW

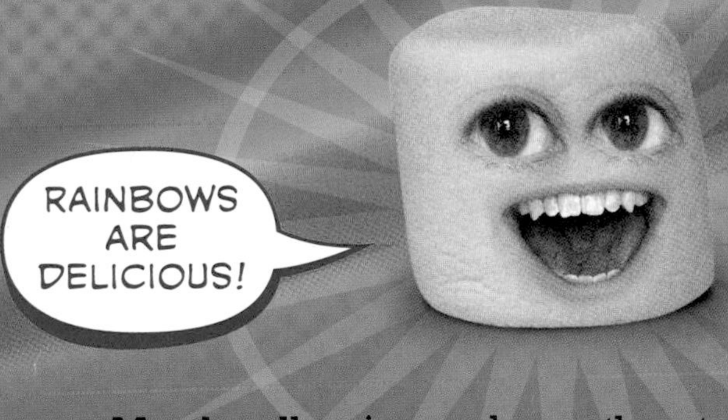
RAINBOWS ARE DELICIOUS!

Marshmallow is a real sweetheart, and it has nothing to do with sugar or gelatin! Marshmallow is made with sunshine, rainbows, and fun! There's even a rumor that Marshmallow's part unicorn. YAY! Danger never seems to bother Marshmallow. Even when roasted Marshmallow only felt "gooey"! Marshmallow truly is sweetness incarnate… YAY!

GRANDPA LEMON

Grandpa Lemon is by far the oldest fruit around. He's also the sleepiest. At odd times he will drift off and... zzzzzzz... fall asleep. Grandpa Lemon is a bit hard of hearing at times and forgetful. By falling asleep and forgetting Orange's jokes, he's capable of annoying Orange! Despite his narcolepsy, being sliced, juiced, made into lemonade, he's little worse for wear. Which only proves that any way you slice him, Grandpa Lemon is here to stay!

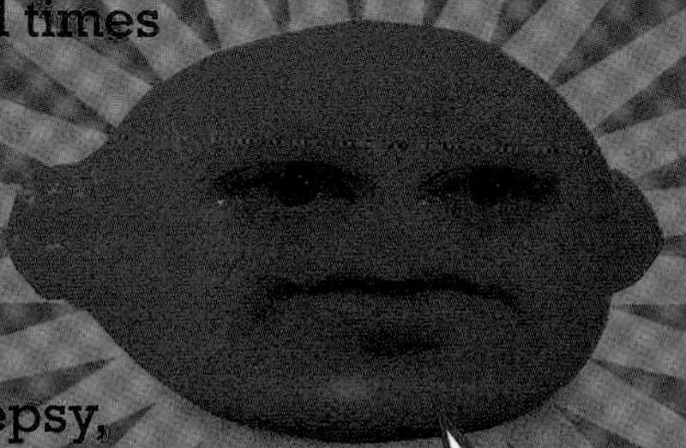
WHAT?! WHO ARE YOU?

GRAPEFRUIT

He's fit, he's firm, he's flexing! That's Grapefruit—a cranky, bad-tempered, tightfisted fruit. When he's not flirting with female fruits, Grapefruit is boasting about his muscles. When he's not breaking a sweat, he's breaking your bones! And if he's not breaking bones, he's breaking hearts! OH!

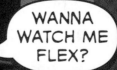

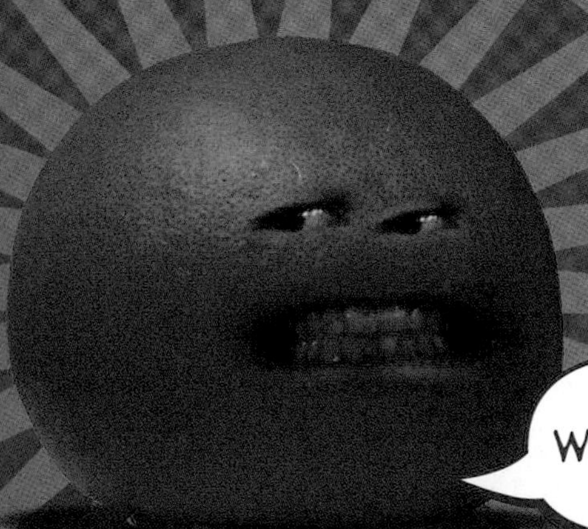
WANNA WATCH ME FLEX?

APPLE

A friend of Orange's but he's constantly annoyed by Orange's jokes, puns, and stories. He often loses his temper when Orange refuses to be quiet. Apple is not a big fan of knives.

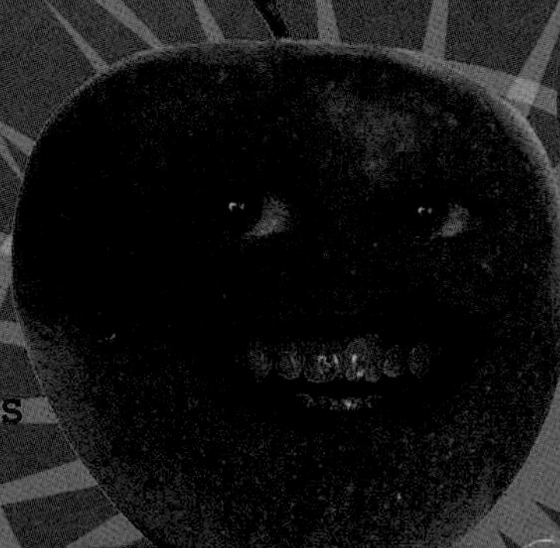
WHAT? WHAT? WHAT IS IT?!

ONE FINE DAY IN THE PRODUCE SECTION

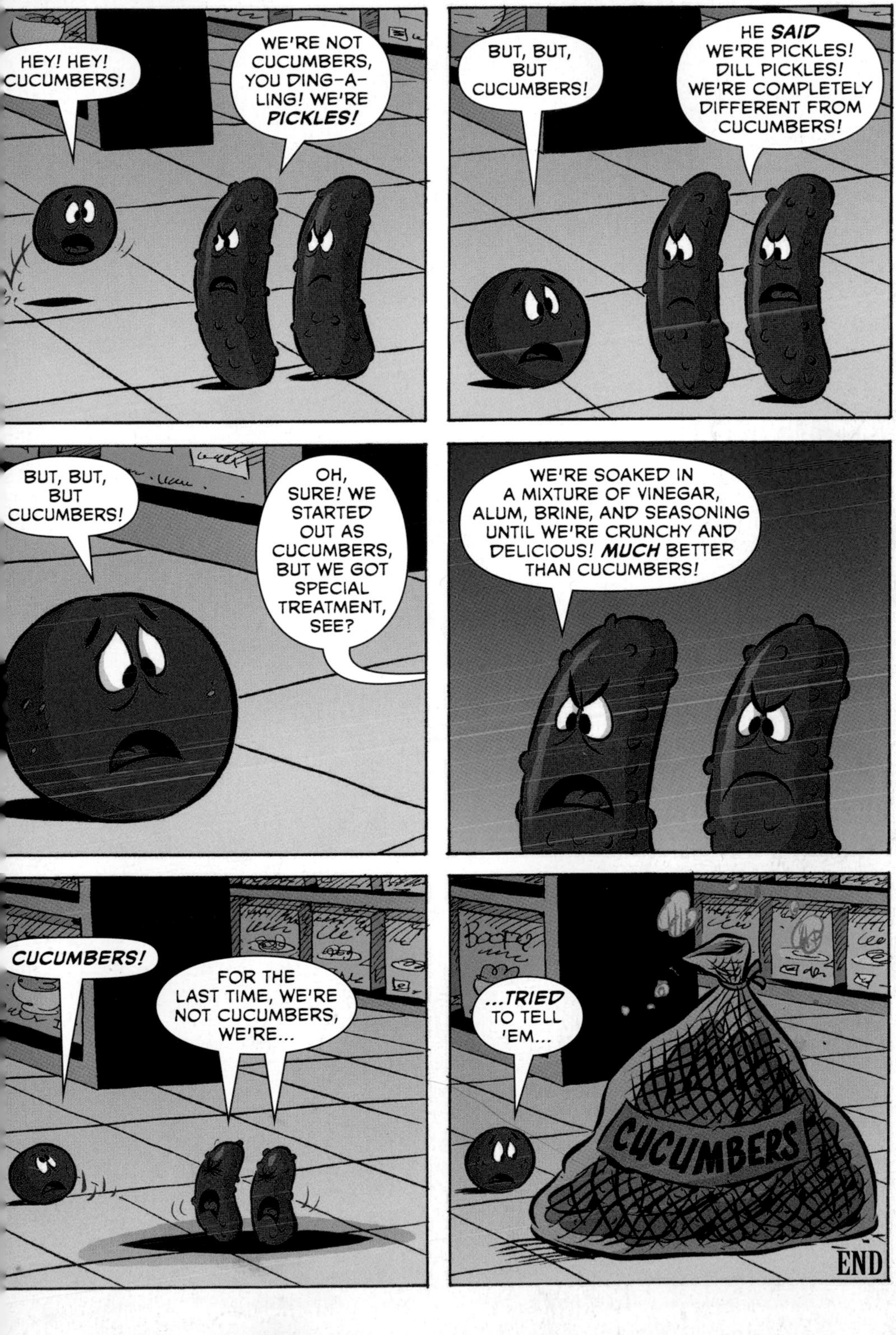
HEY! HEY! CUCUMBERS!
WE'RE NOT CUCUMBERS, YOU DING-A-LING! WE'RE *PICKLES!*
BUT, BUT, BUT CUCUMBERS!
HE *SAID* WE'RE PICKLES! DILL PICKLES! WE'RE COMPLETELY DIFFERENT FROM CUCUMBERS!
BUT, BUT, BUT CUCUMBERS!
OH, SURE! WE STARTED OUT AS CUCUMBERS, BUT WE GOT SPECIAL TREATMENT, SEE?
WE'RE SOAKED IN A MIXTURE OF VINEGAR, ALUM, BRINE, AND SEASONING UNTIL WE'RE CRUNCHY AND DELICIOUS! *MUCH* BETTER THAN CUCUMBERS!
CUCUMBERS!
FOR THE LAST TIME, WE'RE NOT CUCUMBERS, WE'RE...
...*TRIED* TO TELL 'EM...
CUCUMBERS
END

Nerville, The Ladies' Ma

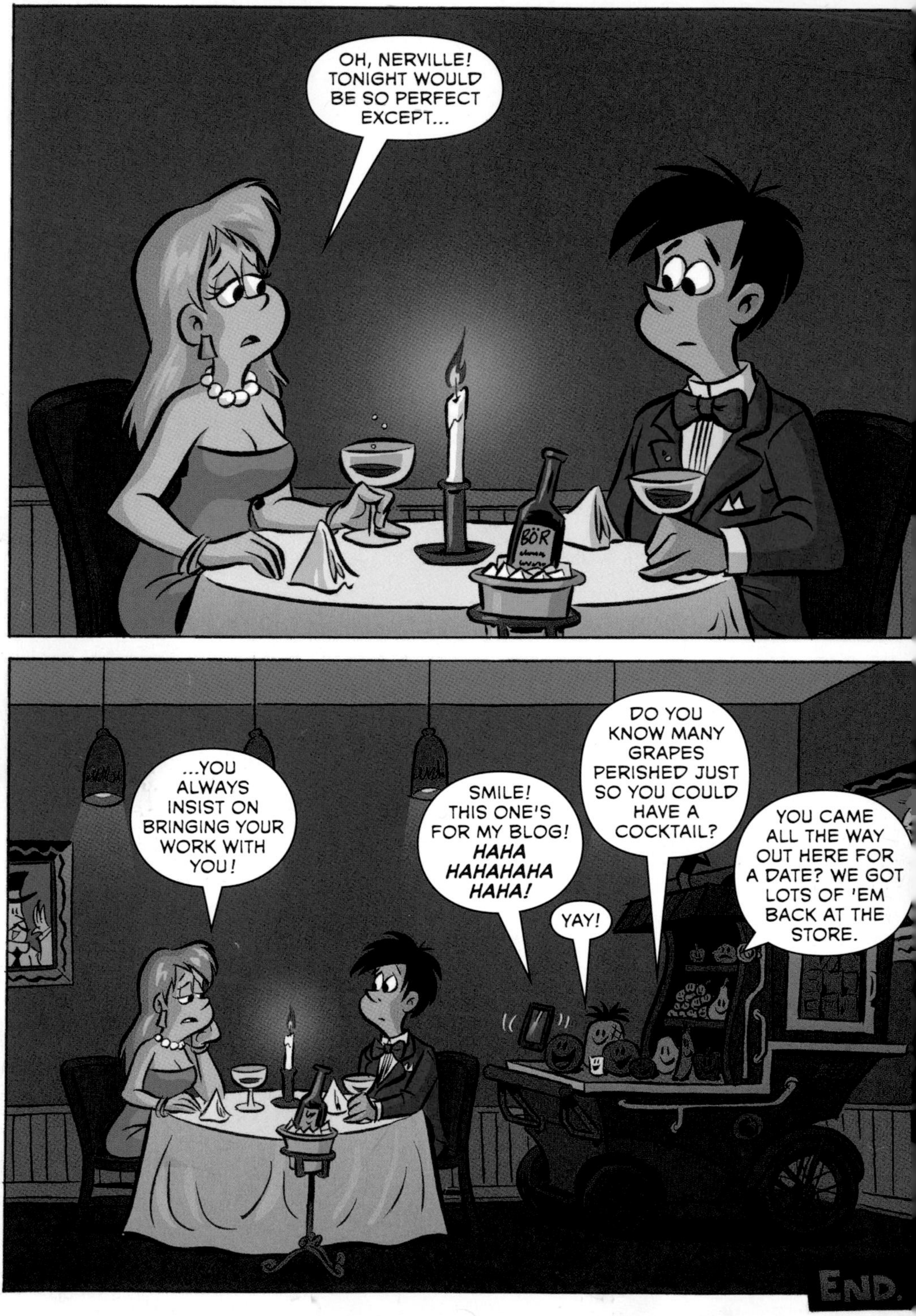
OH, NERVILLE! TONIGHT WOULD BE SO PERFECT EXCEPT...
BÖR
...YOU ALWAYS INSIST ON BRINGING YOUR WORK WITH YOU!
SMILE! THIS ONE'S FOR MY BLOG! **HAHA HAHAHAHA HAHA!**
YAY!
DO YOU KNOW MANY GRAPES PERISHED JUST SO YOU COULD HAVE A COCKTAIL?
YOU CAME ALL THE WAY OUT HERE FOR A DATE? WE GOT LOTS OF 'EM BACK AT THE STORE.
END.

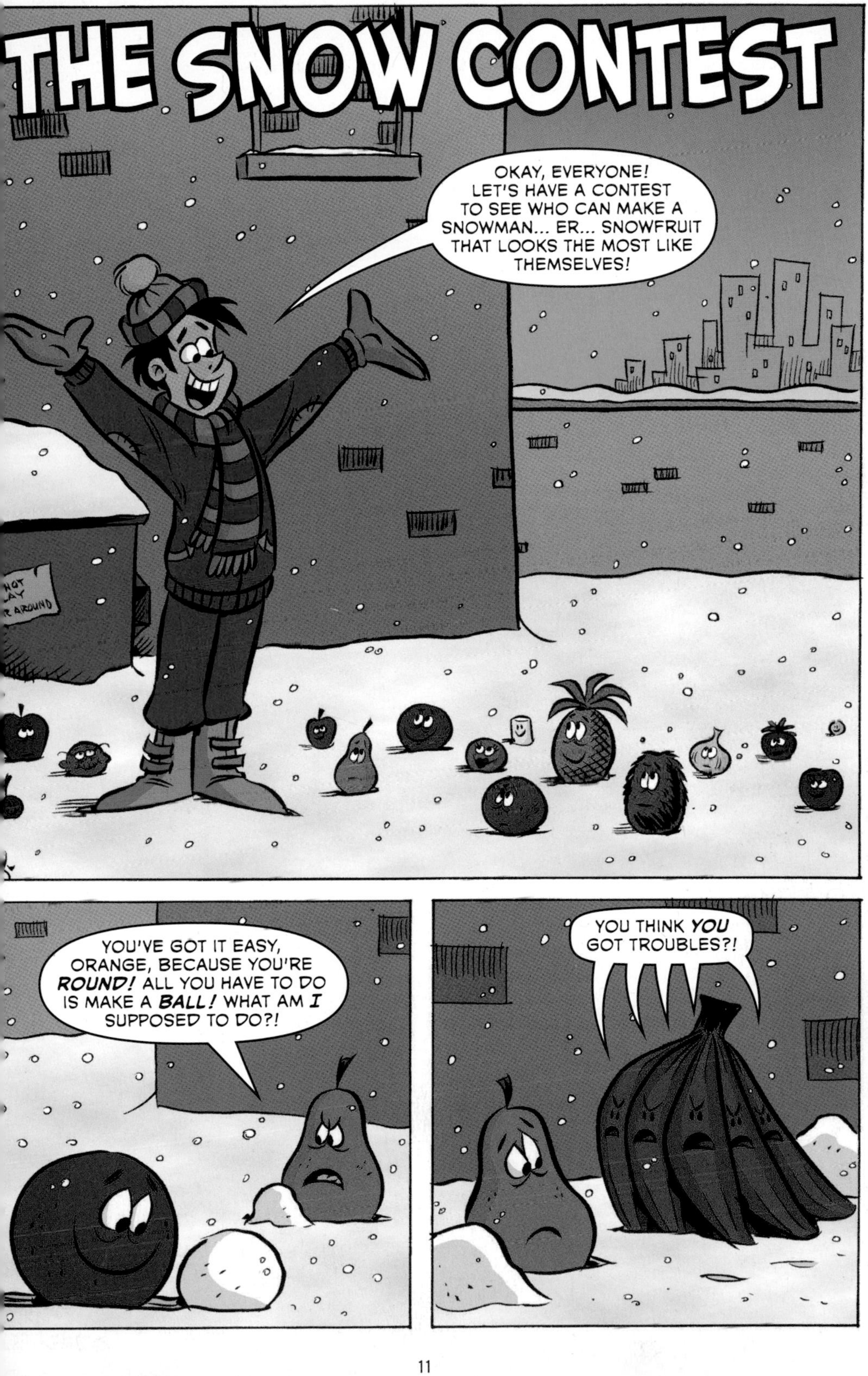
THE SNOW CONTEST
OKAY, EVERYONE! LET'S HAVE A CONTEST TO SEE WHO CAN MAKE A SNOWMAN... ER... SNOWFRUIT THAT LOOKS THE MOST LIKE THEMSELVES!
YOU'VE GOT IT EASY, ORANGE, BECAUSE YOU'RE ROUND! ALL YOU HAVE TO DO IS MAKE A BALL! WHAT AM I SUPPOSED TO DO?!
YOU THINK YOU GOT TROUBLES?!

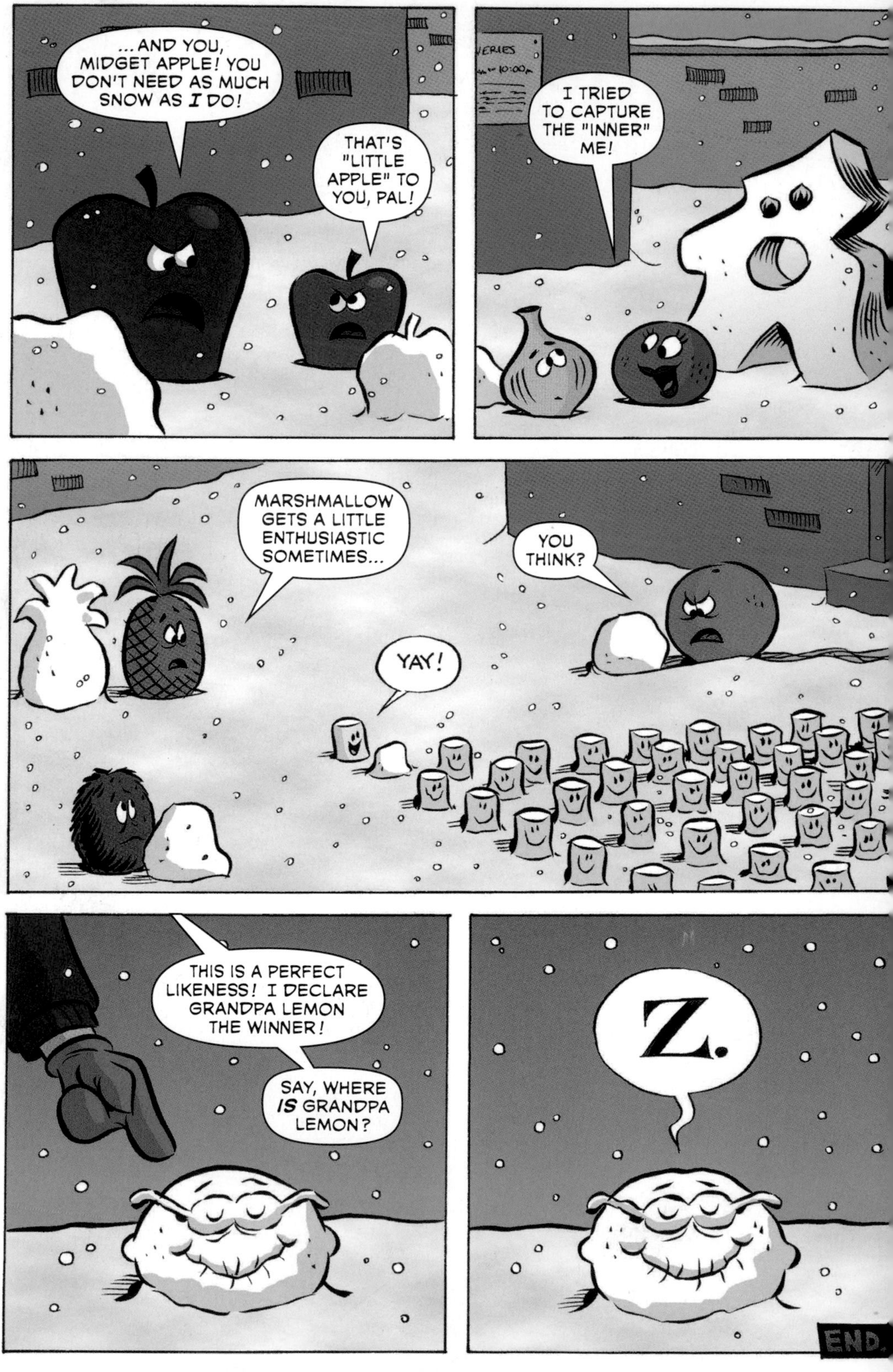

...AND YOU, MIDGET APPLE! YOU DON'T NEED AS MUCH SNOW AS *I* DO!
THAT'S "LITTLE APPLE" TO YOU, PAL!
I TRIED TO CAPTURE THE "INNER" ME!
MARSHMALLOW GETS A LITTLE ENTHUSIASTIC SOMETIMES...
YOU THINK?
YAY!
THIS IS A PERFECT LIKENESS! I DECLARE GRANDPA LEMON THE WINNER!
SAY, WHERE *IS* GRANDPA LEMON?
Z.
END.

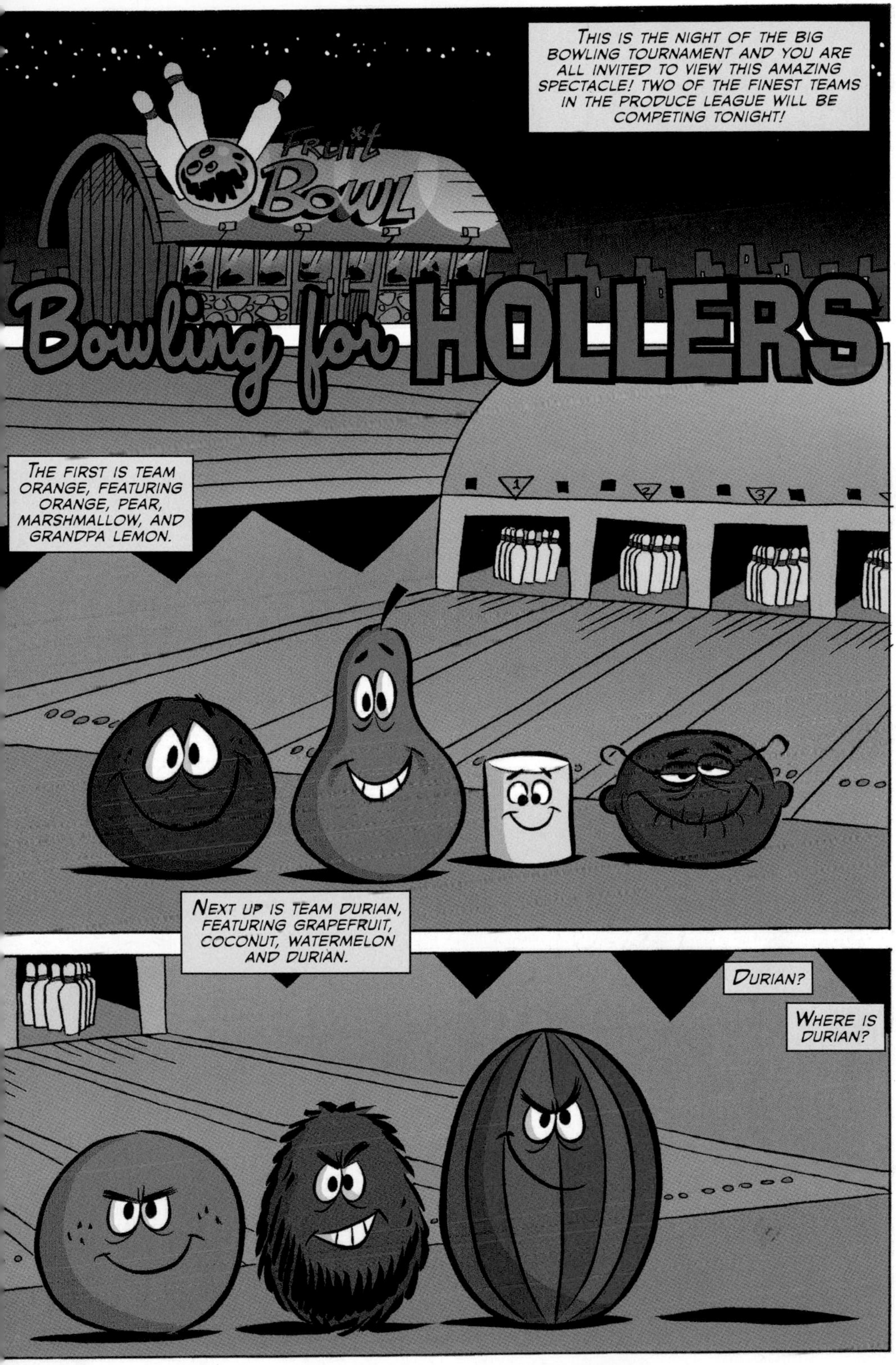
THIS IS THE NIGHT OF THE BIG BOWLING TOURNAMENT AND YOU ARE ALL INVITED TO VIEW THIS AMAZING SPECTACLE! TWO OF THE FINEST TEAMS IN THE PRODUCE LEAGUE WILL BE COMPETING TONIGHT!
Fruit Bowl
Bowling for HOLLERS
THE FIRST IS TEAM ORANGE, FEATURING ORANGE, PEAR, MARSHMALLOW, AND GRANDPA LEMON.
1
2
3
NEXT UP IS TEAM DURIAN, FEATURING GRAPEFRUIT, COCONUT, WATERMELON AND DURIAN.
DURIAN?
WHERE IS DURIAN?

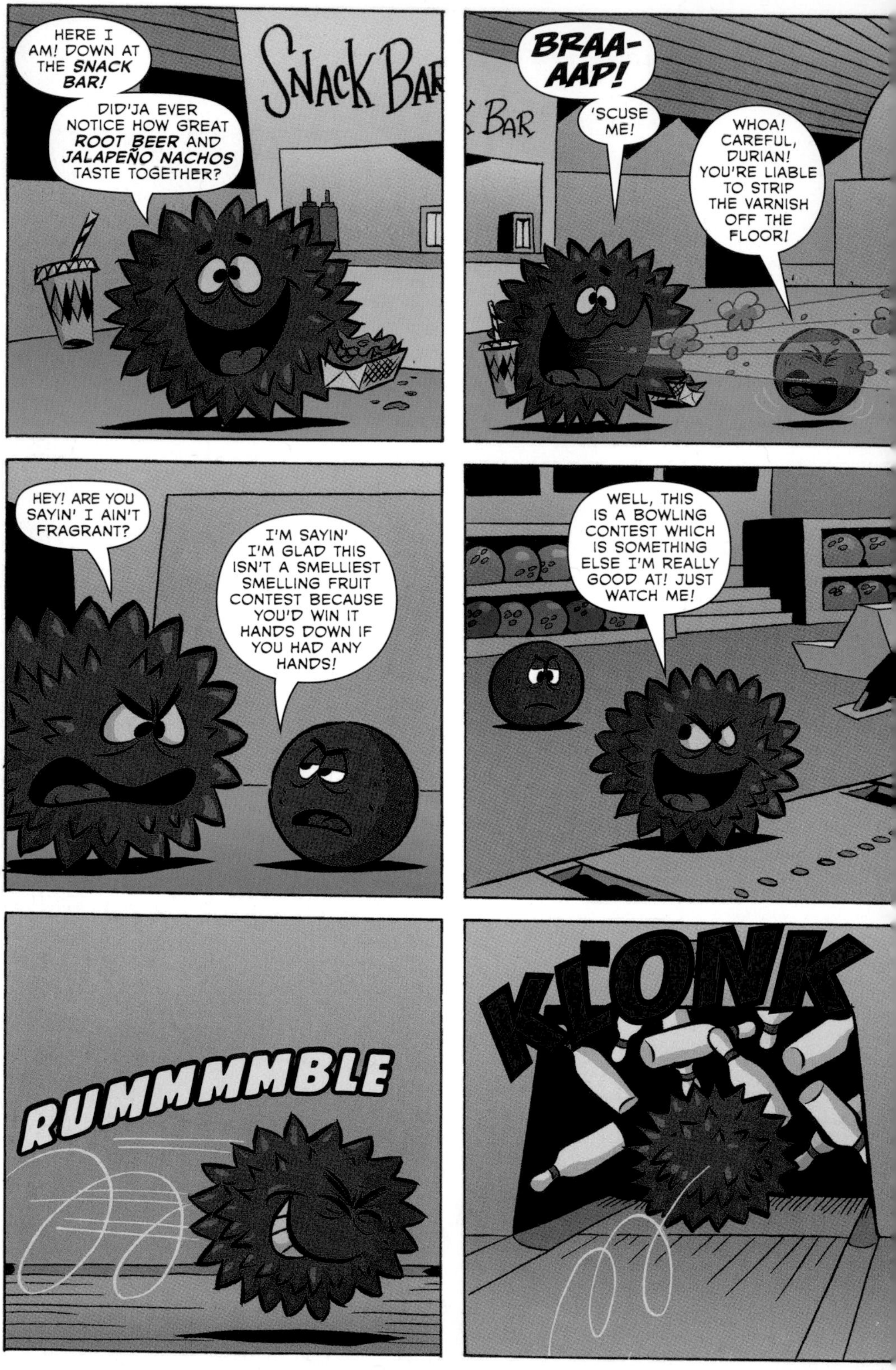
HERE I AM! DOWN AT THE SNACK BAR!
DID'JA EVER NOTICE HOW GREAT ROOT BEER AND JALAPEÑO NACHOS TASTE TOGETHER?
SNACK BAR
BRAAA-AAP!
'SCUSE ME!
WHOA! CAREFUL, DURIAN! YOU'RE LIABLE TO STRIP THE VARNISH OFF THE FLOOR!
HEY! ARE YOU SAYIN' I AIN'T FRAGRANT?
I'M SAYIN' I'M GLAD THIS ISN'T A SMELLIEST SMELLING FRUIT CONTEST BECAUSE YOU'D WIN IT HANDS DOWN IF YOU HAD ANY HANDS!
WELL, THIS IS A BOWLING CONTEST WHICH IS SOMETHING ELSE I'M REALLY GOOD AT! JUST WATCH ME!
RUMMMMBLE
KLONK

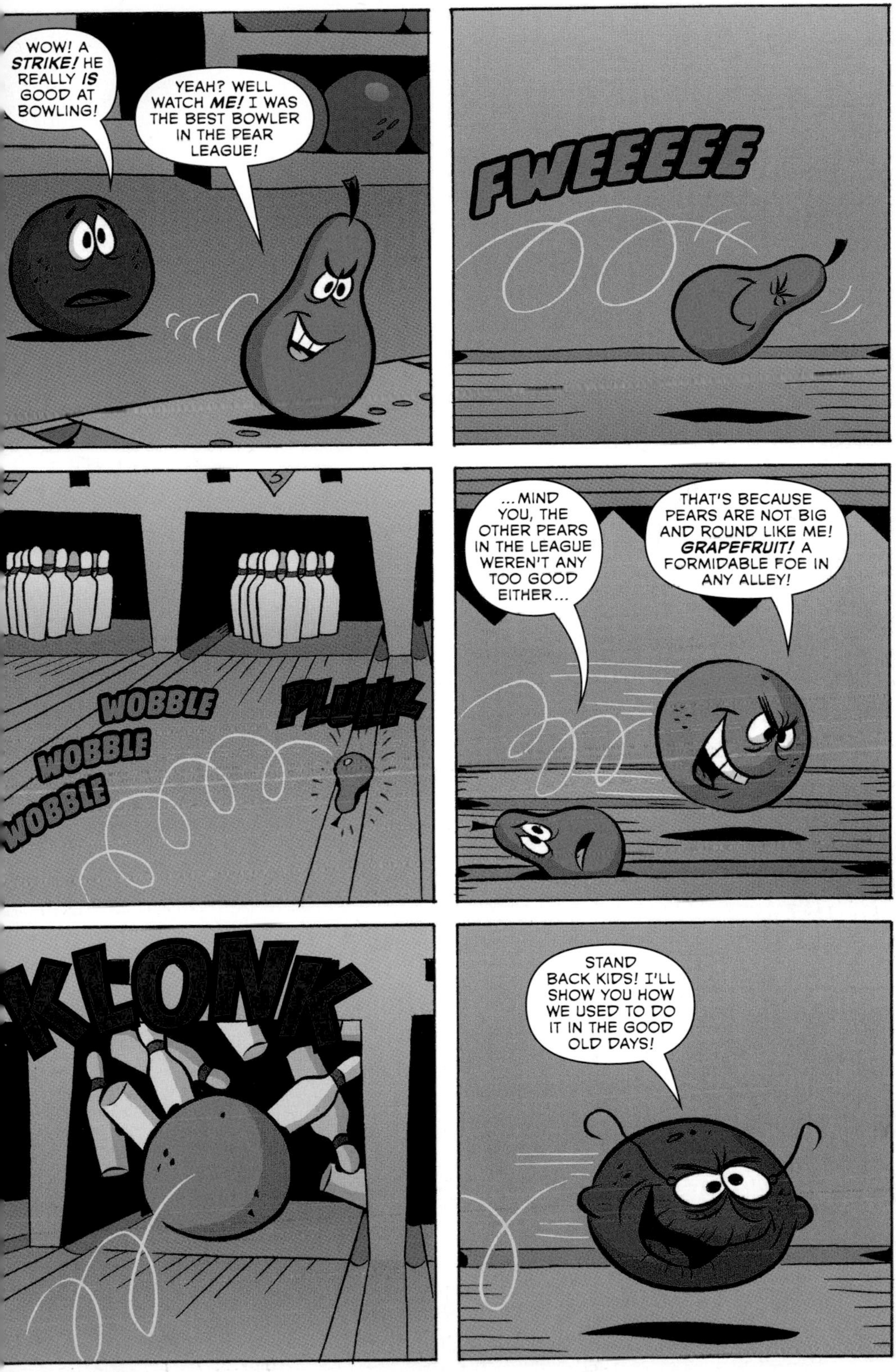
WOW! A STRIKE! HE REALLY IS GOOD AT BOWLING!
YEAH? WELL WATCH ME! I WAS THE BEST BOWLER IN THE PEAR LEAGUE!
FWEEEEEE
WOBBLE
WOBBLE
WOBBLE
PLUNK
...MIND YOU, THE OTHER PEARS IN THE LEAGUE WEREN'T ANY TOO GOOD EITHER...
THAT'S BECAUSE PEARS ARE NOT BIG AND ROUND LIKE ME! GRAPEFRUIT! A FORMIDABLE FOE IN ANY ALLEY!
KLONK
STAND BACK KIDS! I'LL SHOW YOU HOW WE USED TO DO IT IN THE GOOD OLD DAYS!

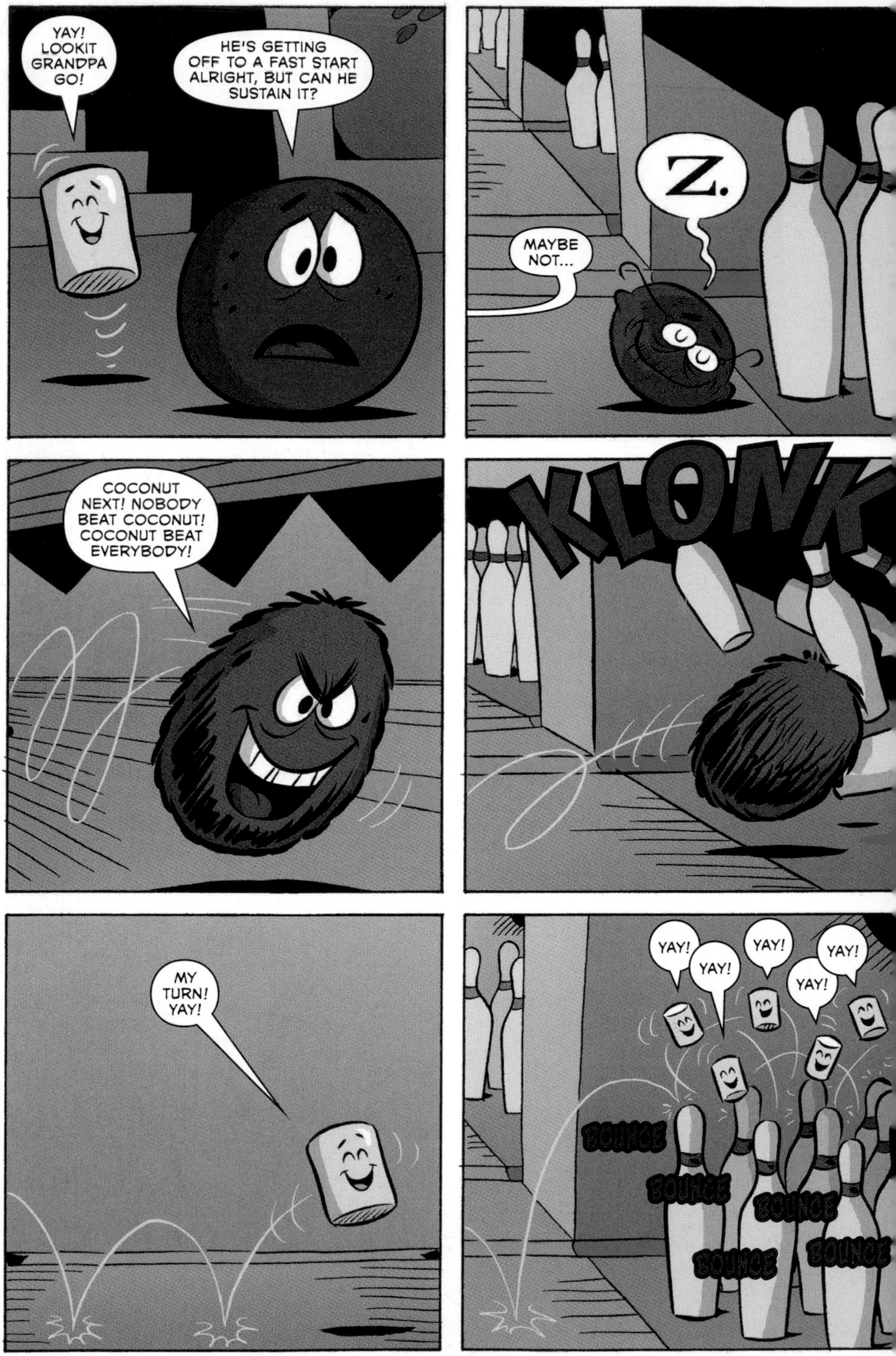
YAY! LOOKIT GRANDPA GO!
HE'S GETTING OFF TO A FAST START ALRIGHT, BUT CAN HE SUSTAIN IT?
Z.
MAYBE NOT...
COCONUT NEXT! NOBODY BEAT COCONUT! COCONUT BEAT EVERYBODY!
KLONK
MY TURN! YAY!
YAY!
YAY!
YAY!
YAY!
YAY!
BOUNCE
BOUNCE
BOUNCE
BOUNCE
BOUNCE

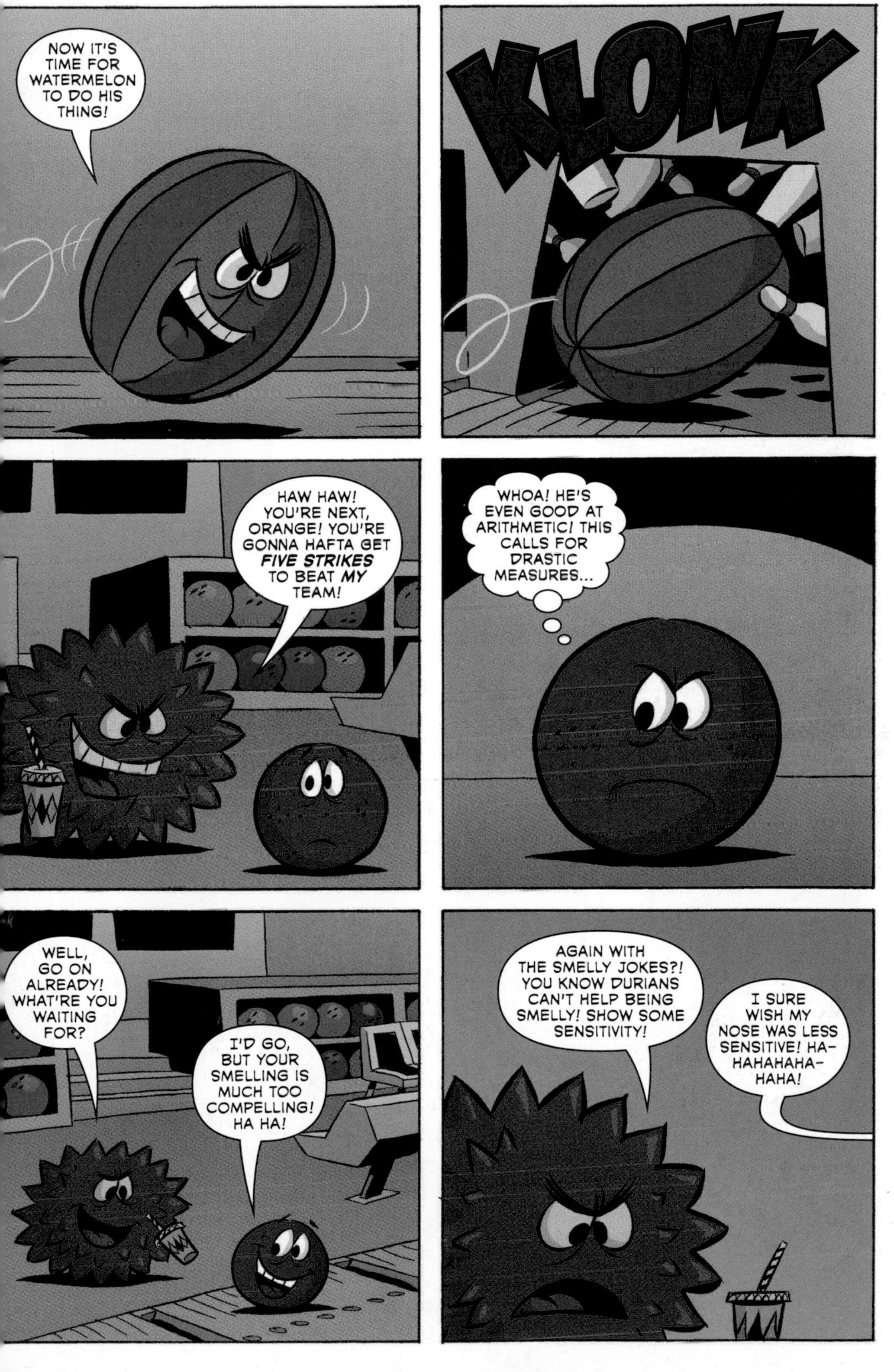
NOW IT'S TIME FOR WATERMELON TO DO HIS THING!
KLONK
HAW HAW! YOU'RE NEXT, ORANGE! YOU'RE GONNA HAFTA GET FIVE STRIKES TO BEAT MY TEAM!
WHOA! HE'S EVEN GOOD AT ARITHMETIC! THIS CALLS FOR DRASTIC MEASURES...
WELL, GO ON ALREADY! WHAT'RE YOU WAITING FOR?
I'D GO, BUT YOUR SMELLING IS MUCH TOO COMPELLING! HA HA!
AGAIN WITH THE SMELLY JOKES?! YOU KNOW DURIANS CAN'T HELP BEING SMELLY! SHOW SOME SENSITIVITY!
I SURE WISH MY NOSE WAS LESS SENSITIVE! HA-HAHAHAHA-HAHA!

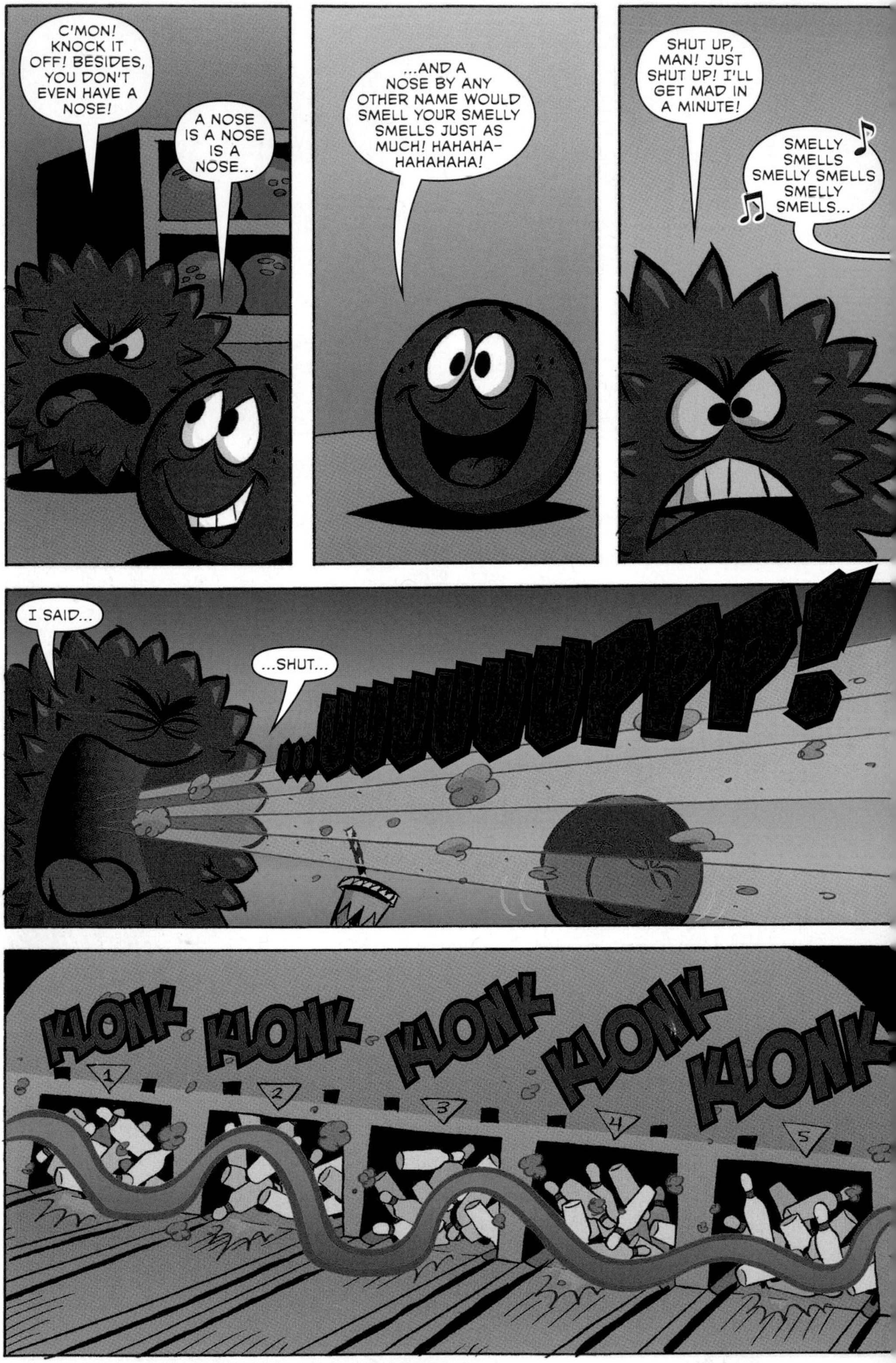
C'MON! KNOCK IT OFF! BESIDES, YOU DON'T EVEN HAVE A NOSE!
A NOSE IS A NOSE IS A NOSE...
...AND A NOSE BY ANY OTHER NAME WOULD SMELL YOUR SMELLY SMELLS JUST AS MUCH! HAHAHA-HAHAHAHA!
SHUT UP, MAN! JUST SHUT UP! I'LL GET MAD IN A MINUTE!
SMELLY SMELLS SMELLY SMELLS SMELLY SMELLS...
I SAID...
...SHUT...
...UUUUUUUPPPP!
KLONK KLONK KLONK KLONK KLONK
1
2
3
4
5

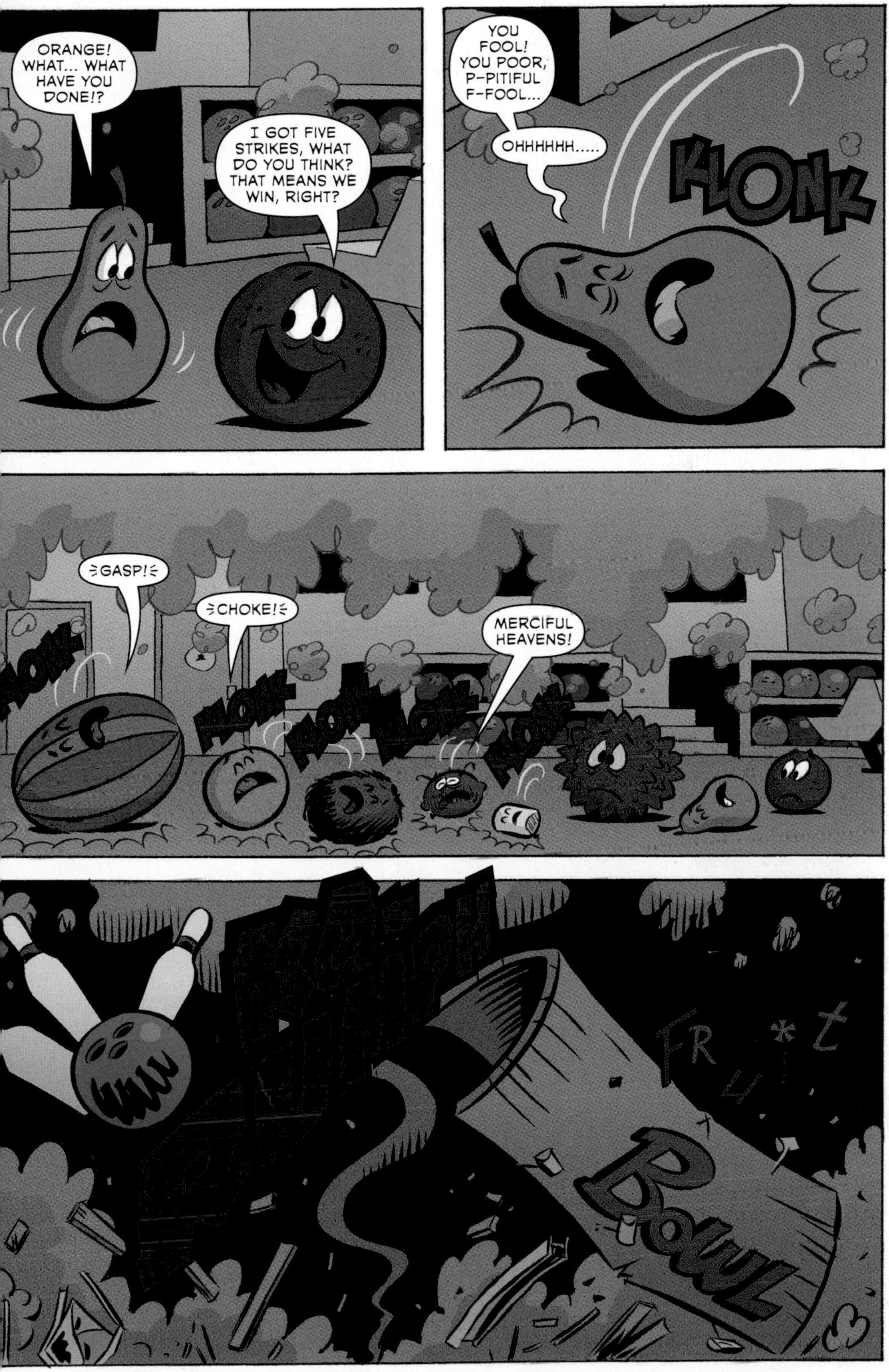
ORANGE! WHAT... WHAT HAVE YOU DONE!?
I GOT FIVE STRIKES, WHAT DO YOU THINK? THAT MEANS WE WIN, RIGHT?
YOU FOOL! YOU POOR, P-PITIFUL F-FOOL...
OHHHHHH.....
KLONK
GASP!
CHOKE!
MERCIFUL HEAVENS!
BOWL

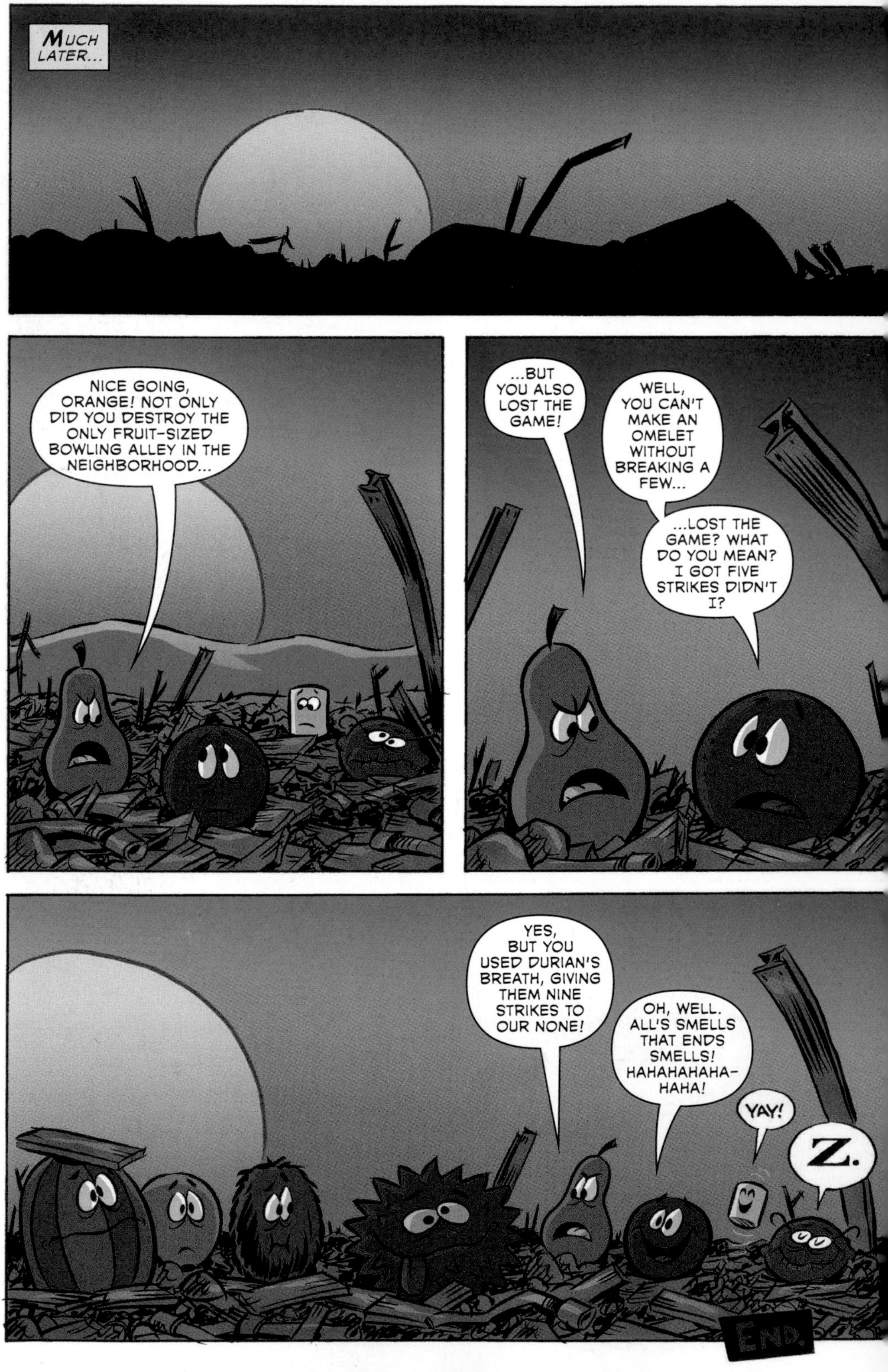
MUCH LATER...
NICE GOING, ORANGE! NOT ONLY DID YOU DESTROY THE ONLY FRUIT-SIZED BOWLING ALLEY IN THE NEIGHBORHOOD...
...BUT YOU ALSO LOST THE GAME!
WELL, YOU CAN'T MAKE AN OMELET WITHOUT BREAKING A FEW...
...LOST THE GAME? WHAT DO YOU MEAN? I GOT FIVE STRIKES DIDN'T I?
YES, BUT YOU USED DURIAN'S BREATH, GIVING THEM NINE STRIKES TO OUR NONE!
OH, WELL. ALL'S SMELLS THAT ENDS SMELLS! HAHAHAHAHA-HAHA!
YAY!
Z.
END.

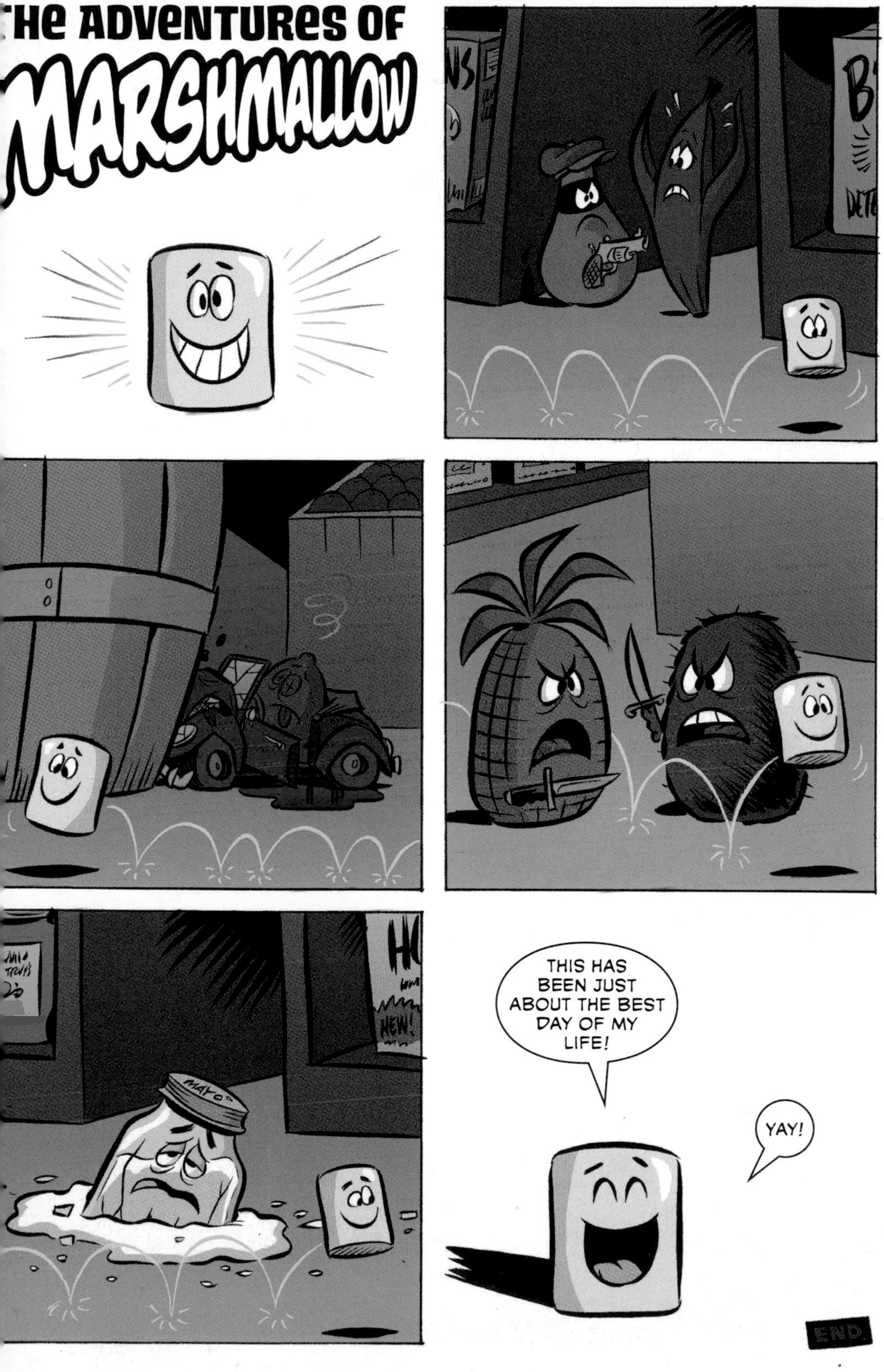
THE ADVENTURES OF
MARSHMALLOW
MAYO
THIS HAS BEEN JUST ABOUT THE BEST DAY OF MY LIFE!
YAY!
END

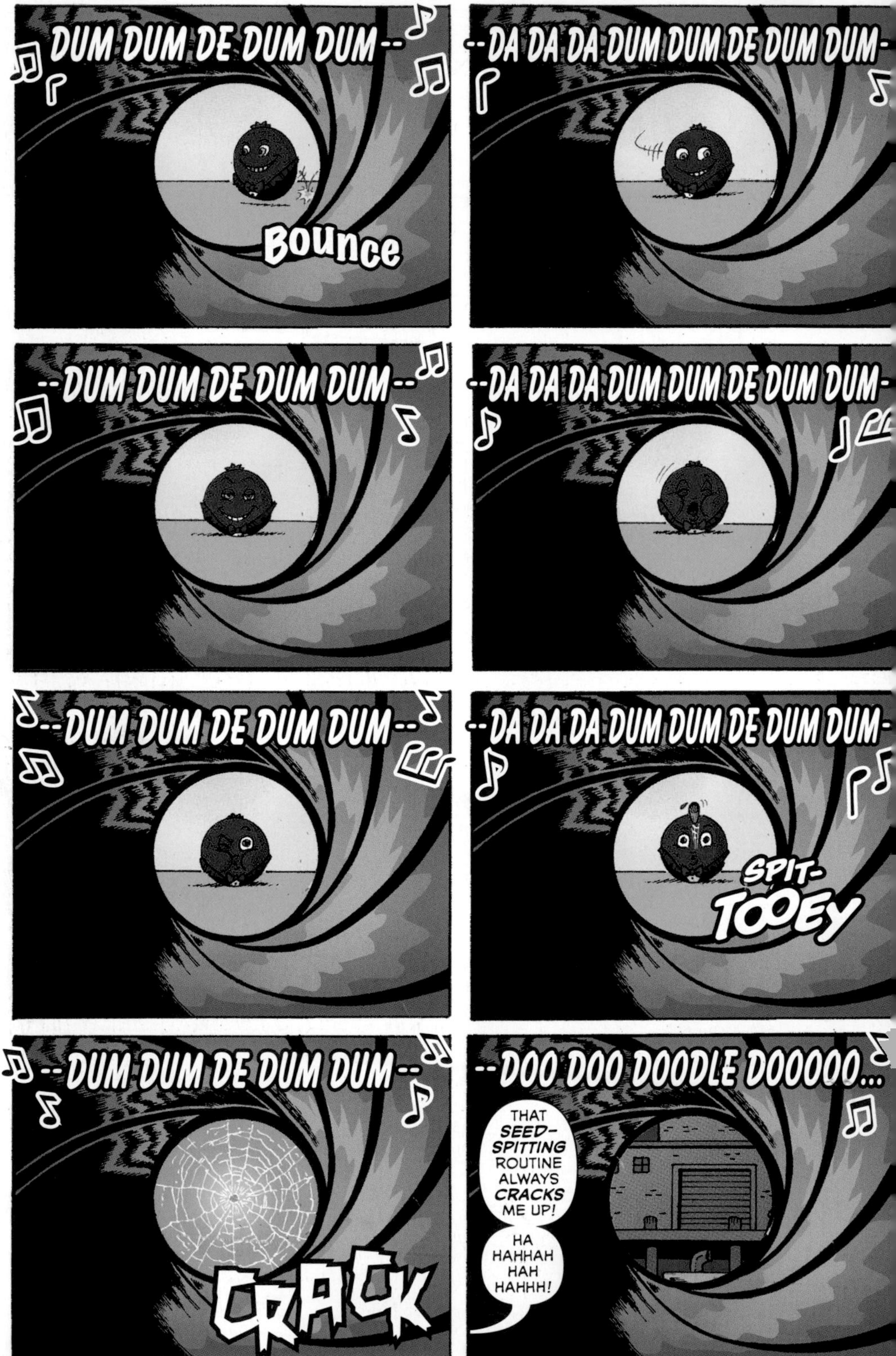
DUM DUM DE DUM DUM--
Bounce
--DA DA DA DUM DUM DE DUM DUM-
--DUM DUM DE DUM DUM--
--DA DA DA DUM DUM DE DUM DUM-
--DUM DUM DE DUM DUM--
--DA DA DA DUM DUM DE DUM DUM-
SPIT-TOOEY
--DUM DUM DE DUM DUM--
CRACK
--DOO DOO DOODLE DOOOOO...
THAT SEED-SPITTING ROUTINE ALWAYS CRACKS ME UP!
HA HAHHAH HAH HAHHH!

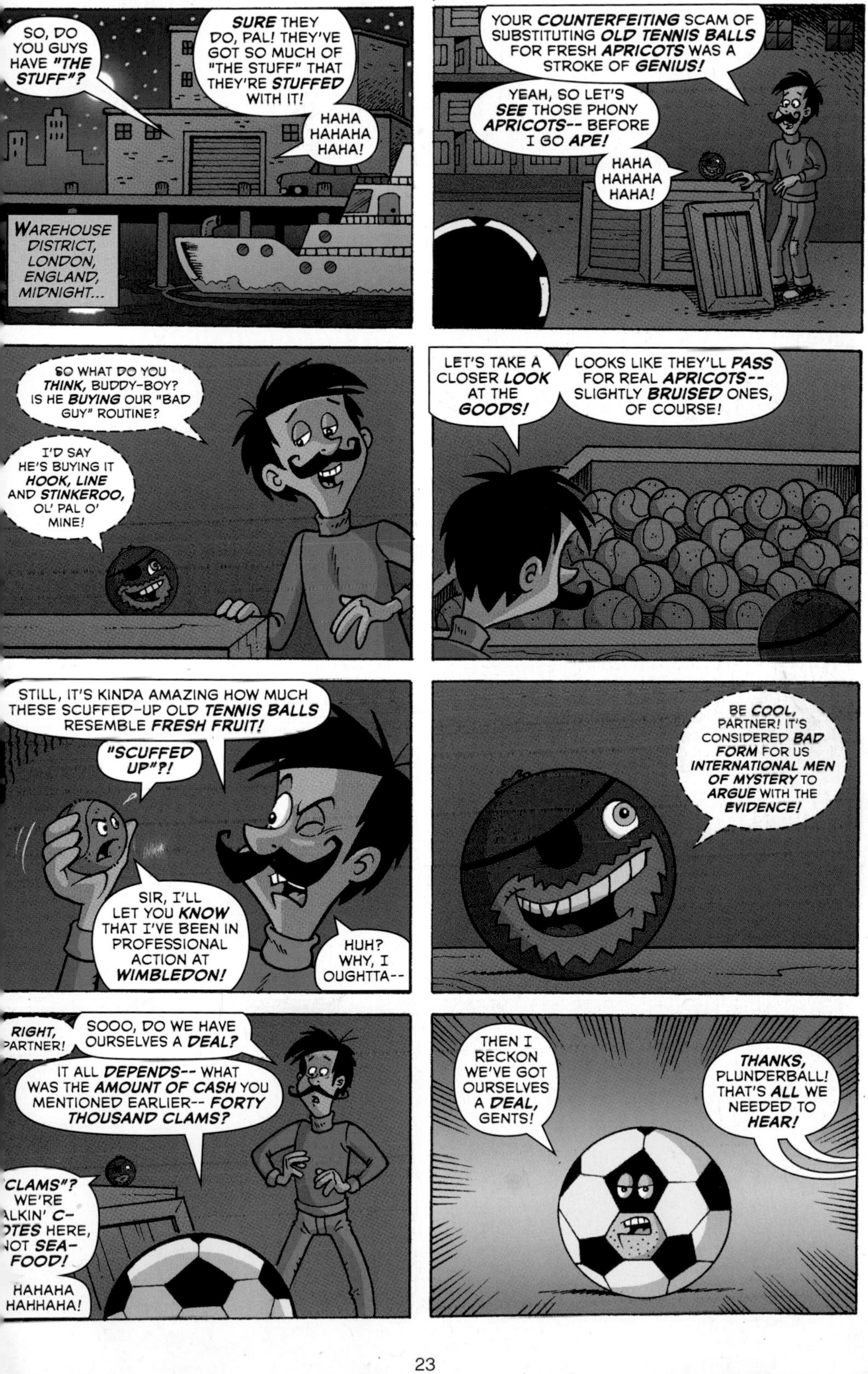
SO, DO YOU GUYS HAVE "THE STUFF"?
SURE THEY DO, PAL! THEY'VE GOT SO MUCH OF "THE STUFF" THAT THEY'RE STUFFED WITH IT!
HAHA HAHAHA HAHA!
WAREHOUSE DISTRICT, LONDON, ENGLAND, MIDNIGHT...
YOUR COUNTERFEITING SCAM OF SUBSTITUTING OLD TENNIS BALLS FOR FRESH APRICOTS WAS A STROKE OF GENIUS!
YEAH, SO LET'S SEE THOSE PHONY APRICOTS-- BEFORE I GO APE!
HAHA HAHAHA HAHA!
SO WHAT DO YOU THINK, BUDDY-BOY? IS HE BUYING OUR "BAD GUY" ROUTINE?
I'D SAY HE'S BUYING IT HOOK, LINE AND STINKEROO, OL' PAL O' MINE!
LET'S TAKE A CLOSER LOOK AT THE GOODS!
LOOKS LIKE THEY'LL PASS FOR REAL APRICOTS-- SLIGHTLY BRUISED ONES, OF COURSE!
STILL, IT'S KINDA AMAZING HOW MUCH THESE SCUFFED-UP OLD TENNIS BALLS RESEMBLE FRESH FRUIT!
"SCUFFED UP"?!
SIR, I'LL LET YOU KNOW THAT I'VE BEEN IN PROFESSIONAL ACTION AT WIMBLEDON!
HUH? WHY, I OUGHTTA--
BE COOL, PARTNER! IT'S CONSIDERED BAD FORM FOR US INTERNATIONAL MEN OF MYSTERY TO ARGUE WITH THE EVIDENCE!
RIGHT, PARTNER!
SOOO, DO WE HAVE OURSELVES A DEAL?
IT ALL DEPENDS-- WHAT WAS THE AMOUNT OF CASH YOU MENTIONED EARLIER-- FORTY THOUSAND CLAMS?
"CLAMS"? WE'RE TALKIN' C-NOTES HERE, NOT SEA-FOOD!
HAHAHA HAHHAHA!
THEN I RECKON WE'VE GOT OURSELVES A DEAL, GENTS!
THANKS, PLUNDERBALL! THAT'S ALL WE NEEDED TO HEAR!

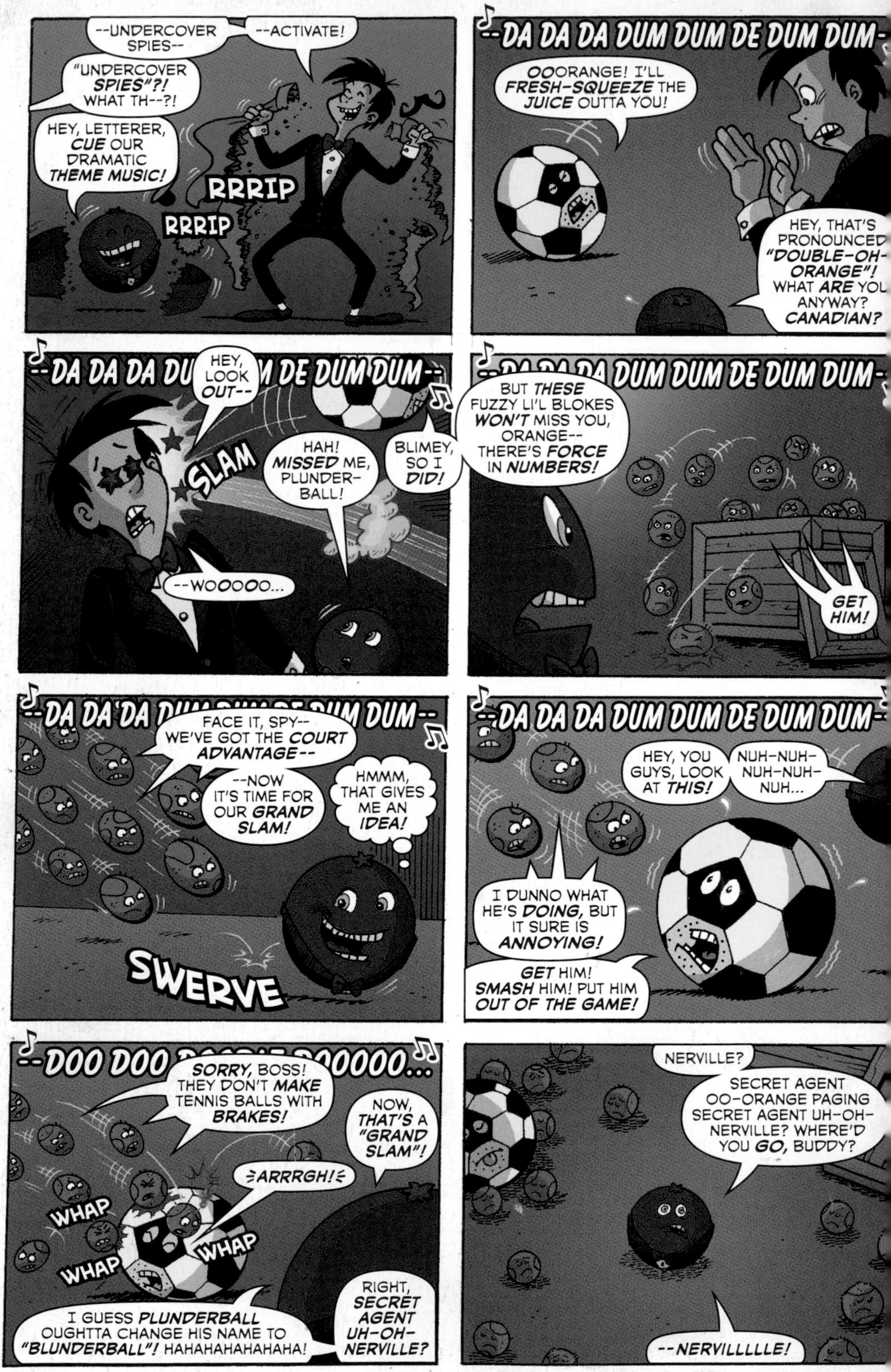
--UNDERCOVER SPIES--
--ACTIVATE!
"UNDERCOVER SPIES"?! WHAT TH--?!
HEY, LETTERER, CUE OUR DRAMATIC THEME MUSIC!
RRRIP
RRRIP
--DA DA DA DUM DUM DE DUM DUM--
OOORANGE! I'LL FRESH-SQUEEZE THE JUICE OUTTA YOU!
HEY, THAT'S PRONOUNCED "DOUBLE-OH-ORANGE"! WHAT ARE YOU ANYWAY? CANADIAN?
HEY, LOOK OUT--
SLAM
--WOOOOO...
HAH! MISSED ME, PLUNDER-BALL!
BLIMEY, SO I DID!
BUT THESE FUZZY LI'L BLOKES WON'T MISS YOU, ORANGE-- THERE'S FORCE IN NUMBERS!
GET HIM!
FACE IT, SPY-- WE'VE GOT THE COURT ADVANTAGE--
--NOW IT'S TIME FOR OUR GRAND SLAM!
HMMM, THAT GIVES ME AN IDEA!
SWERVE
--DA DA DA DUM DUM DE DUM DUM--
HEY, YOU GUYS, LOOK AT THIS!
NUH-NUH-NUH-NUH-NUH...
I DUNNO WHAT HE'S DOING, BUT IT SURE IS ANNOYING!
GET HIM! SMASH HIM! PUT HIM OUT OF THE GAME!
SORRY, BOSS! THEY DON'T MAKE TENNIS BALLS WITH BRAKES!
NOW, THAT'S A "GRAND SLAM"!
ARRRGH!
WHAP
WHAP
WHAP
I GUESS PLUNDERBALL OUGHTTA CHANGE HIS NAME TO "BLUNDERBALL"! HAHAHAHAHAHAHA!
RIGHT, SECRET AGENT UH-OH-NERVILLE?
NERVILLE?
SECRET AGENT OO-ORANGE PAGING SECRET AGENT UH-OH-NERVILLE? WHERE'D YOU GO, BUDDY?
--NERVILLLLLE!

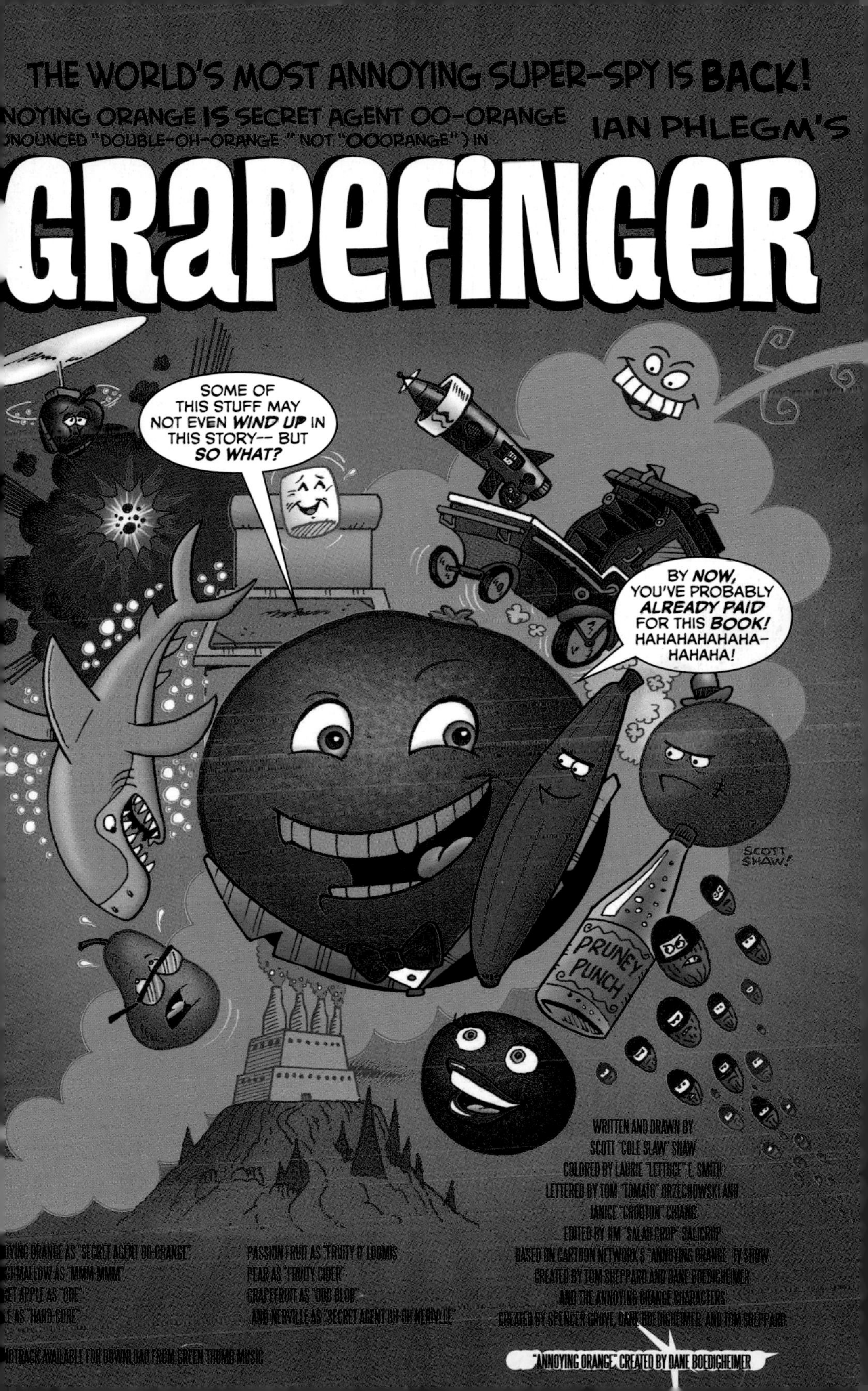
THE WORLD'S MOST ANNOYING SUPER-SPY IS BACK!
NOYING ORANGE IS SECRET AGENT OO-ORANGE
NOUNCED "DOUBLE-OH-ORANGE" NOT "OOORANGE") IN
IAN PHLEGM'S
GRAPEFINGER
SOME OF THIS STUFF MAY NOT EVEN WIND UP IN THIS STORY-- BUT SO WHAT?
BY NOW, YOU'VE PROBABLY ALREADY PAID FOR THIS BOOK! HAHAHAHAHAHA-HAHAHA!
SCOTT SHAW!
PRUNEY PUNCH
WRITTEN AND DRAWN BY
SCOTT "COLE SLAW" SHAW
COLORED BY LAURIE "LETTUCE" E. SMITH
LETTERED BY TOM "TOMATO" ORZECHOWSKI AND
JANICE "CROUTON" CHIANG
EDITED BY JIM "SALAD CROP" SALICRUP
BASED ON CARTOON NETWORK'S "ANNOYING ORANGE" TV SHOW
CREATED BY TOM SHEPPARD AND DANE BOEDIGHEIMER
AND THE ANNOYING ORANGE CHARACTERS
CREATED BY SPENCER GROVE, DANE BOEDIGHEIMER, AND TOM SHEPPARD
YING ORANGE AS "SECRET AGENT OO-ORANGE"
GHMALLOW AS "MMM-MMM"
GET APPLE AS "ODE"
LE AS "HARD-CORE"
PASSION FRUIT AS "FRUITY O' LOOMIS
PEAR AS "FRUITY CIDER"
GRAPEFRUIT AS "ODD BLOB"
AND NERVILLE AS "SECRET AGENT UH-OH NERVILLE"
DTRACK AVAILABLE FOR DOWNLOAD FROM GREEN THUMB MUSIC
"ANNOYING ORANGE" CREATED BY DANE BOEDIGHEIMER

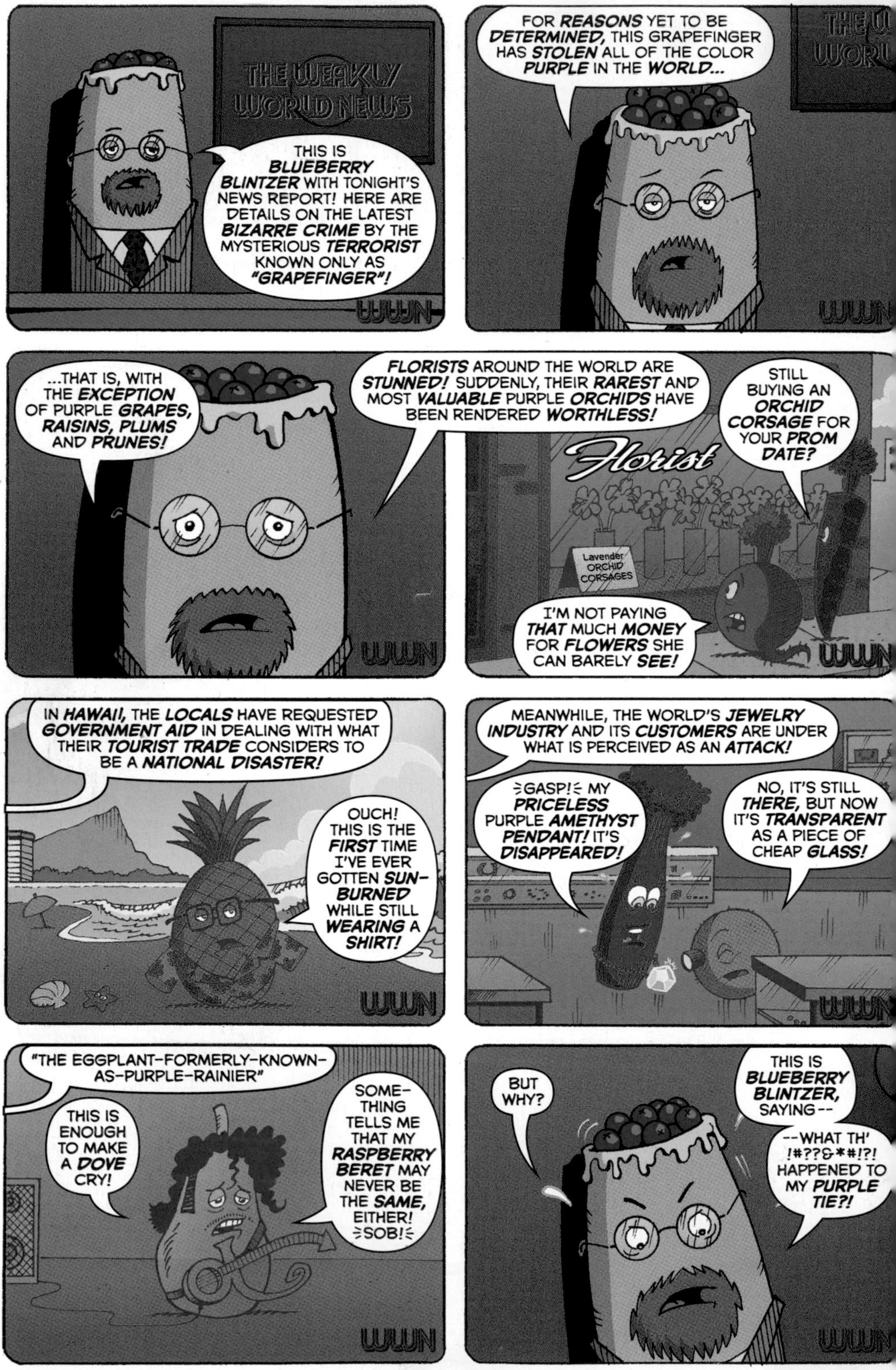
THE WEAKLY WORLD NEWS
THIS IS BLUEBERRY BLINTZER WITH TONIGHT'S NEWS REPORT! HERE ARE DETAILS ON THE LATEST BIZARRE CRIME BY THE MYSTERIOUS TERRORIST KNOWN ONLY AS "GRAPEFINGER"!
WWN
FOR REASONS YET TO BE DETERMINED, THIS GRAPEFINGER HAS STOLEN ALL OF THE COLOR PURPLE IN THE WORLD...
WWN
...THAT IS, WITH THE EXCEPTION OF PURPLE GRAPES, RAISINS, PLUMS AND PRUNES!
WWN
FLORISTS AROUND THE WORLD ARE STUNNED! SUDDENLY, THEIR RAREST AND MOST VALUABLE PURPLE ORCHIDS HAVE BEEN RENDERED WORTHLESS!
Florist
Lavender ORCHID CORSAGES
STILL BUYING AN ORCHID CORSAGE FOR YOUR PROM DATE?
I'M NOT PAYING THAT MUCH MONEY FOR FLOWERS SHE CAN BARELY SEE!
WWN
IN HAWAII, THE LOCALS HAVE REQUESTED GOVERNMENT AID IN DEALING WITH WHAT THEIR TOURIST TRADE CONSIDERS TO BE A NATIONAL DISASTER!
OUCH! THIS IS THE FIRST TIME I'VE EVER GOTTEN SUN-BURNED WHILE STILL WEARING A SHIRT!
WWN
MEANWHILE, THE WORLD'S JEWELRY INDUSTRY AND ITS CUSTOMERS ARE UNDER WHAT IS PERCEIVED AS AN ATTACK!
GASP! MY PRICELESS PURPLE AMETHYST PENDANT! IT'S DISAPPEARED!
NO, IT'S STILL THERE, BUT NOW IT'S TRANSPARENT AS A PIECE OF CHEAP GLASS!
WWN
"THE EGGPLANT-FORMERLY-KNOWN-AS-PURPLE-RAINIER"
THIS IS ENOUGH TO MAKE A DOVE CRY!
SOME-THING TELLS ME THAT MY RASPBERRY BERET MAY NEVER BE THE SAME, EITHER! SOB!
WWN
BUT WHY?
THIS IS BLUEBERRY BLINTZER, SAYING--
--WHAT TH' !#??&*#!?! HAPPENED TO MY PURPLE TIE?!
WWN

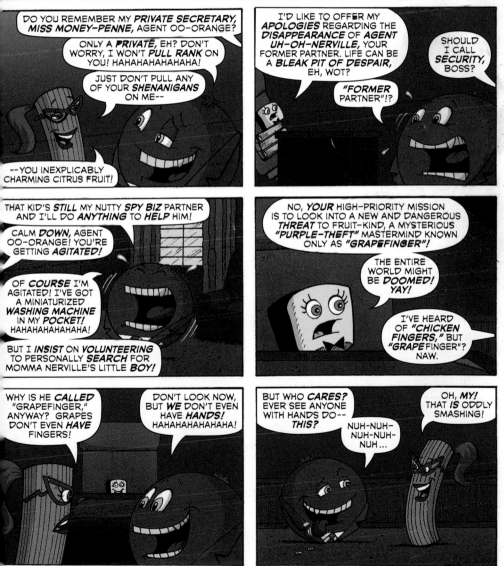

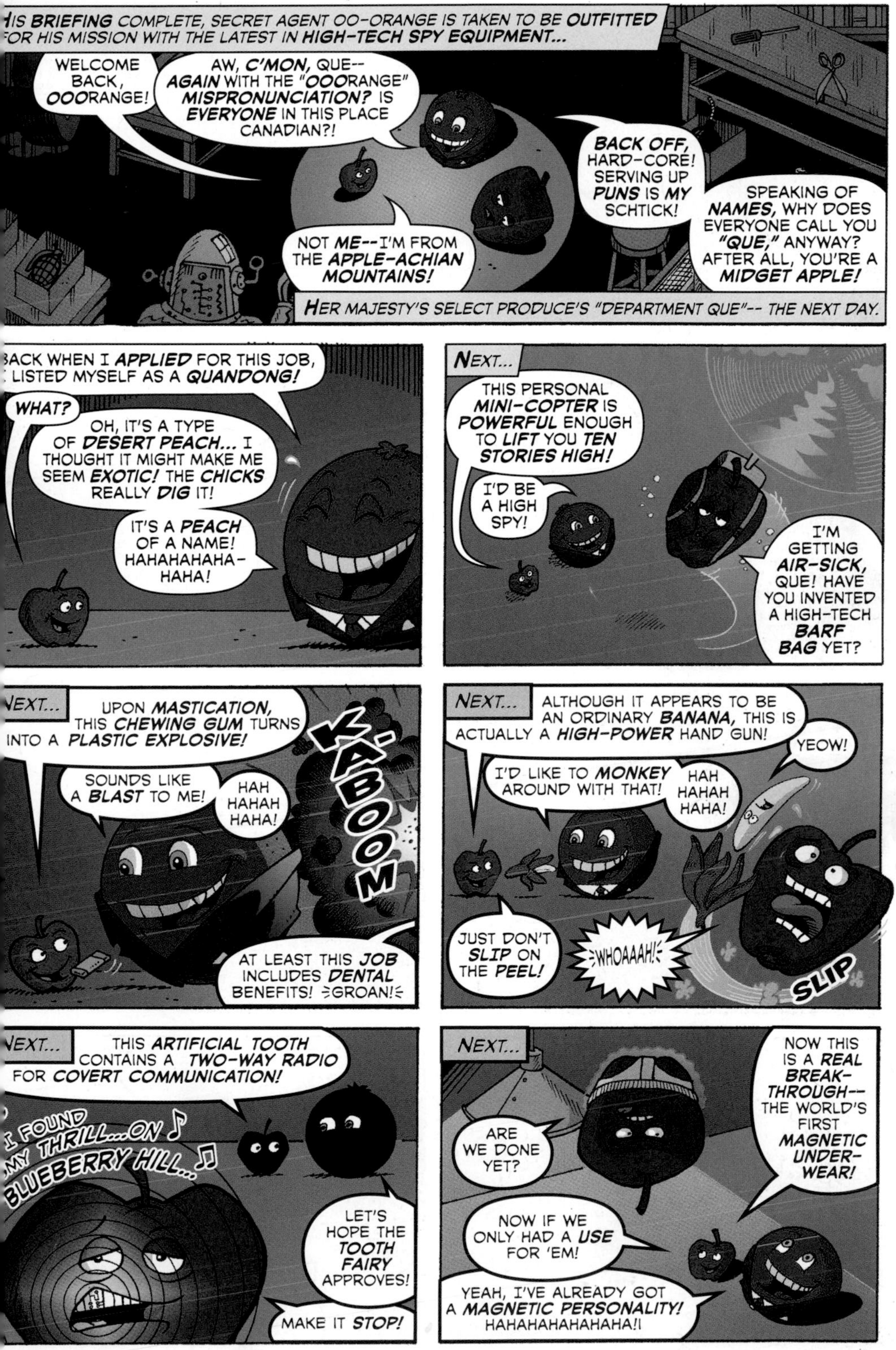
HIS BRIEFING COMPLETE, SECRET AGENT OO-ORANGE IS TAKEN TO BE OUTFITTED FOR HIS MISSION WITH THE LATEST IN HIGH-TECH SPY EQUIPMENT...
WELCOME BACK, OOORANGE!
AW, C'MON, QUE-- AGAIN WITH THE "OOORANGE" MISPRONUNCIATION? IS EVERYONE IN THIS PLACE CANADIAN?!
NOT ME--I'M FROM THE APPLE-ACHIAN MOUNTAINS!
BACK OFF, HARD-CORE! SERVING UP PUNS IS MY SCHTICK!
SPEAKING OF NAMES, WHY DOES EVERYONE CALL YOU "QUE," ANYWAY? AFTER ALL, YOU'RE A MIDGET APPLE!
HER MAJESTY'S SELECT PRODUCE'S "DEPARTMENT QUE"-- THE NEXT DAY.
BACK WHEN I APPLIED FOR THIS JOB, I LISTED MYSELF AS A QUANDONG!
WHAT?
OH, IT'S A TYPE OF DESERT PEACH... I THOUGHT IT MIGHT MAKE ME SEEM EXOTIC! THE CHICKS REALLY DIG IT!
IT'S A PEACH OF A NAME! HAHAHAHAHAHA-HAHA!
NEXT...
THIS PERSONAL MINI-COPTER IS POWERFUL ENOUGH TO LIFT YOU TEN STORIES HIGH!
I'D BE A HIGH SPY!
I'M GETTING AIR-SICK, QUE! HAVE YOU INVENTED A HIGH-TECH BARF BAG YET?
NEXT...
UPON MASTICATION, THIS CHEWING GUM TURNS INTO A PLASTIC EXPLOSIVE!
KA-BOOOM
SOUNDS LIKE A BLAST TO ME!
HAH HAHAH HAHA!
AT LEAST THIS JOB INCLUDES DENTAL BENEFITS! GROAN!
NEXT...
ALTHOUGH IT APPEARS TO BE AN ORDINARY BANANA, THIS IS ACTUALLY A HIGH-POWER HAND GUN!
YEOW!
I'D LIKE TO MONKEY AROUND WITH THAT!
HAH HAHAH HAHA!
JUST DON'T SLIP ON THE PEEL!
WHOAAAH!
SLIP
NEXT...
THIS ARTIFICIAL TOOTH CONTAINS A TWO-WAY RADIO FOR COVERT COMMUNICATION!
I FOUND MY THRILL...ON BLUEBERRY HILL...
LET'S HOPE THE TOOTH FAIRY APPROVES!
MAKE IT STOP!
NEXT...
NOW THIS IS A REAL BREAK-THROUGH-- THE WORLD'S FIRST MAGNETIC UNDER-WEAR!
ARE WE DONE YET?
NOW IF WE ONLY HAD A USE FOR 'EM!
YEAH, I'VE ALREADY GOT A MAGNETIC PERSONALITY! HAHAHAHAHAHAHA!!

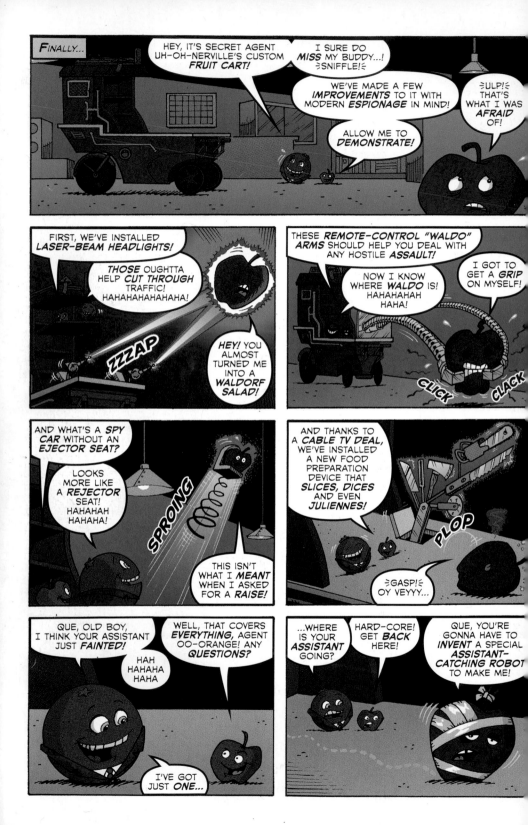

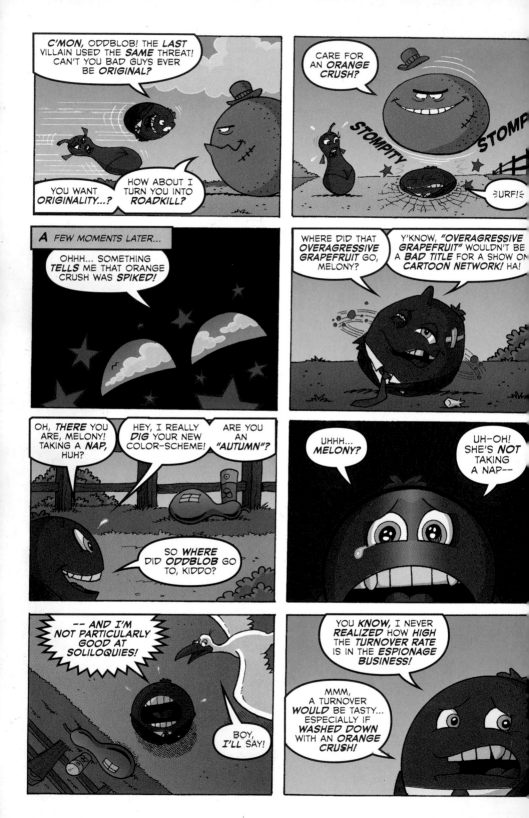

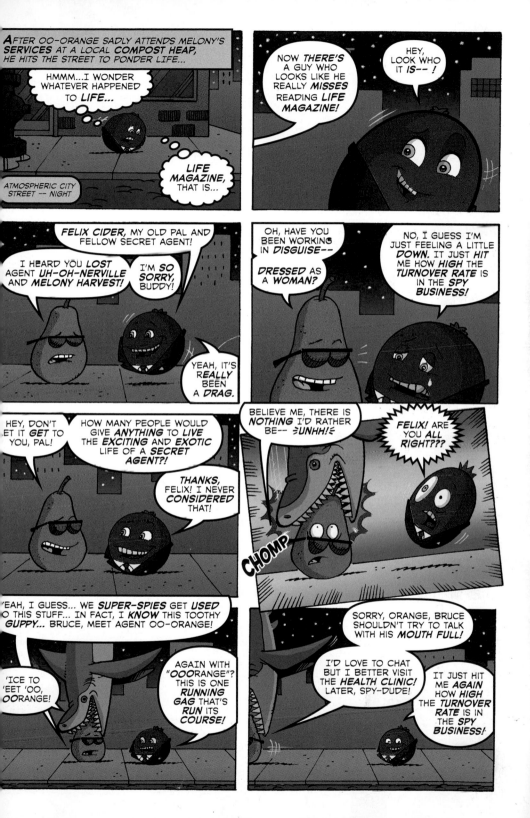

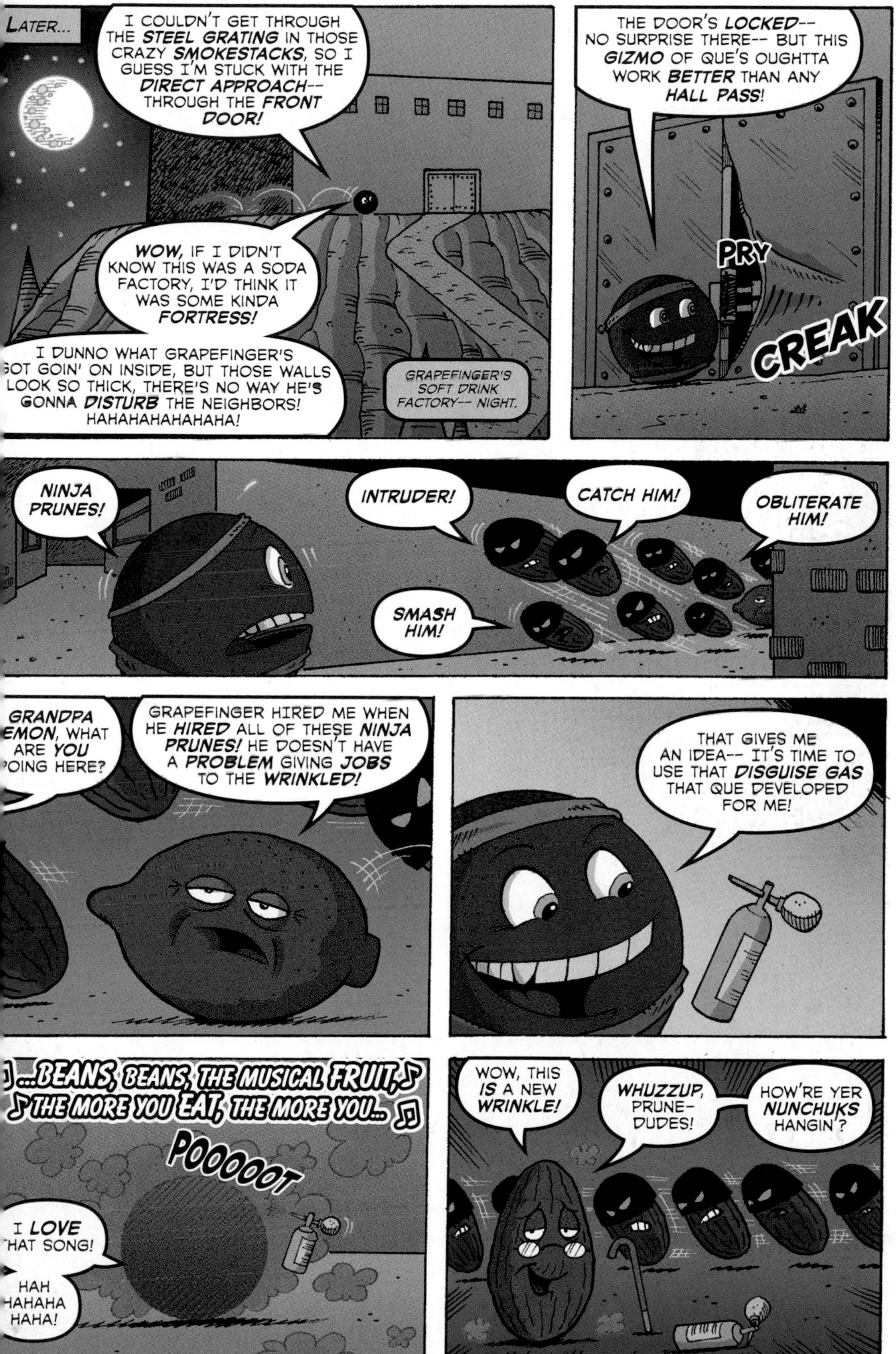

LATER...
I COULDN'T GET THROUGH THE STEEL GRATING IN THOSE CRAZY SMOKESTACKS, SO I GUESS I'M STUCK WITH THE DIRECT APPROACH-- THROUGH THE FRONT DOOR!
WOW, IF I DIDN'T KNOW THIS WAS A SODA FACTORY, I'D THINK IT WAS SOME KINDA FORTRESS!
I DUNNO WHAT GRAPEFINGER'S GOT GOIN' ON INSIDE, BUT THOSE WALLS LOOK SO THICK, THERE'S NO WAY HE'S GONNA DISTURB THE NEIGHBORS! HAHAHAHAHAHAHA!
GRAPEFINGER'S SOFT DRINK FACTORY-- NIGHT.
THE DOOR'S LOCKED-- NO SURPRISE THERE-- BUT THIS GIZMO OF QUE'S OUGHTTA WORK BETTER THAN ANY HALL PASS!
PRY
CREAK
NINJA PRUNES!
INTRUDER!
CATCH HIM!
OBLITERATE HIM!
SMASH HIM!
GRANDPA EMON, WHAT ARE YOU OING HERE?
GRAPEFINGER HIRED ME WHEN HE HIRED ALL OF THESE NINJA PRUNES! HE DOESN'T HAVE A PROBLEM GIVING JOBS TO THE WRINKLED!
THAT GIVES ME AN IDEA-- IT'S TIME TO USE THAT DISGUISE GAS THAT QUE DEVELOPED FOR ME!
♫ ...BEANS, BEANS, THE MUSICAL FRUIT, ♪ ♪ THE MORE YOU EAT, THE MORE YOU... ♫
POOOOOT
I LOVE HAT SONG!
HAH HAHAHA HAHA!
WOW, THIS IS A NEW WRINKLE!
WHUZZUP, PRUNE-DUDES!
HOW'RE YER NUNCHUKS HANGIN'?

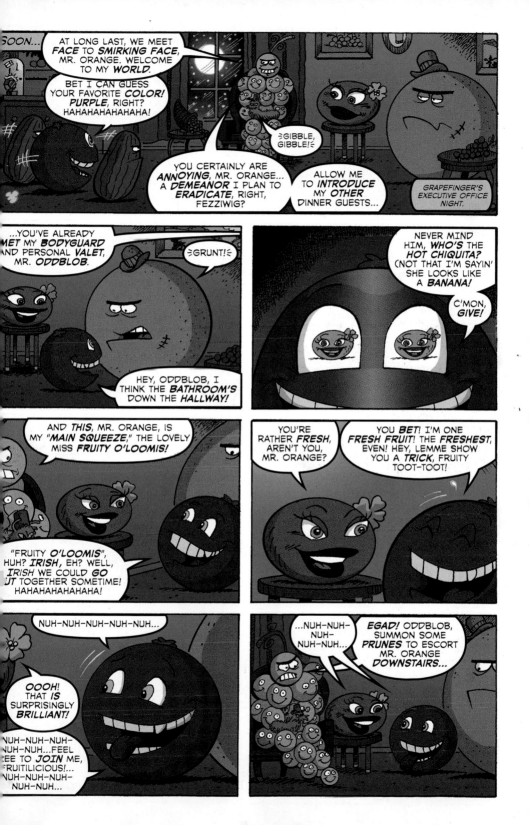

37

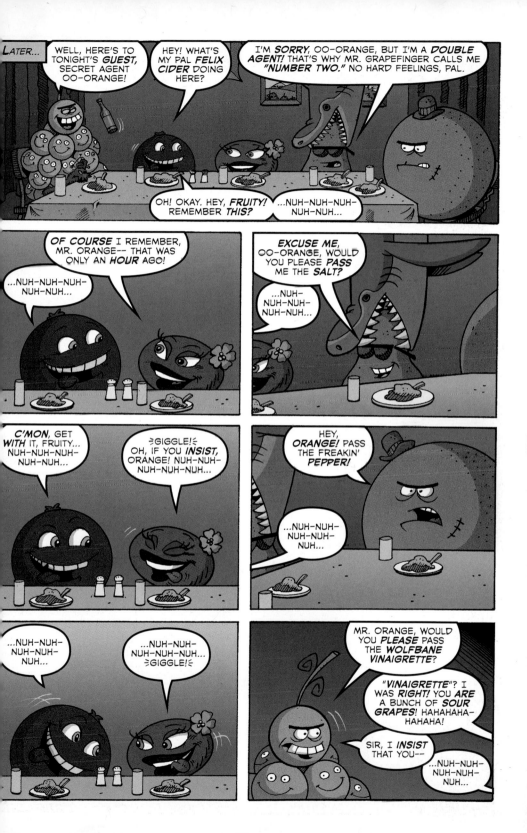

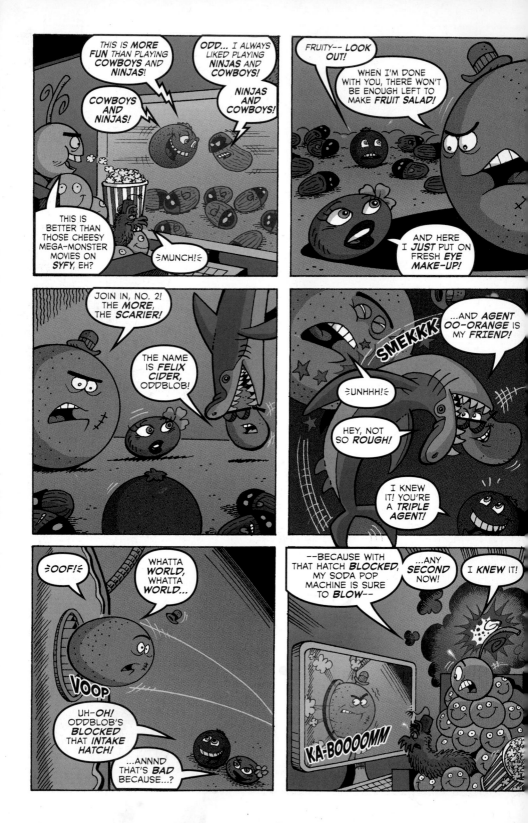

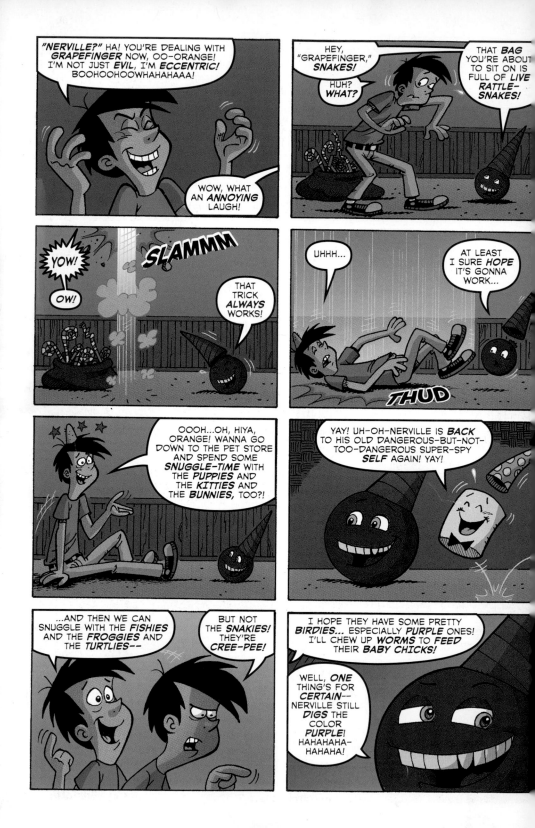

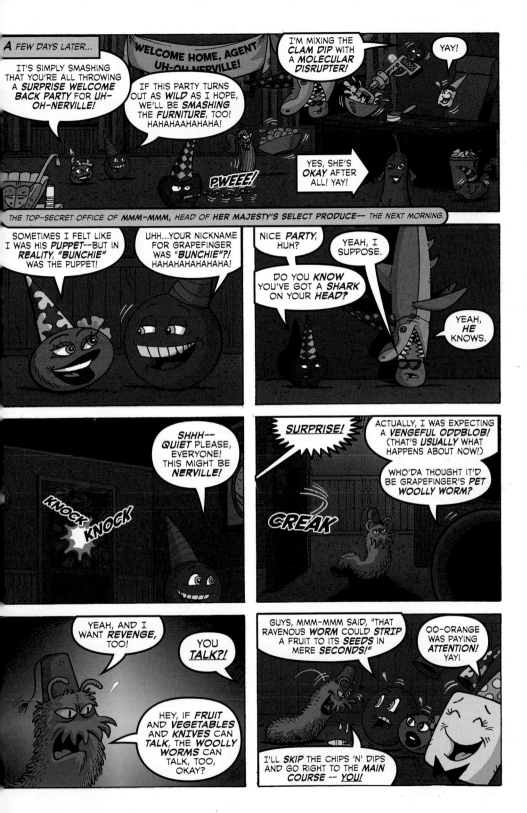

PLUM'S DAY OUT

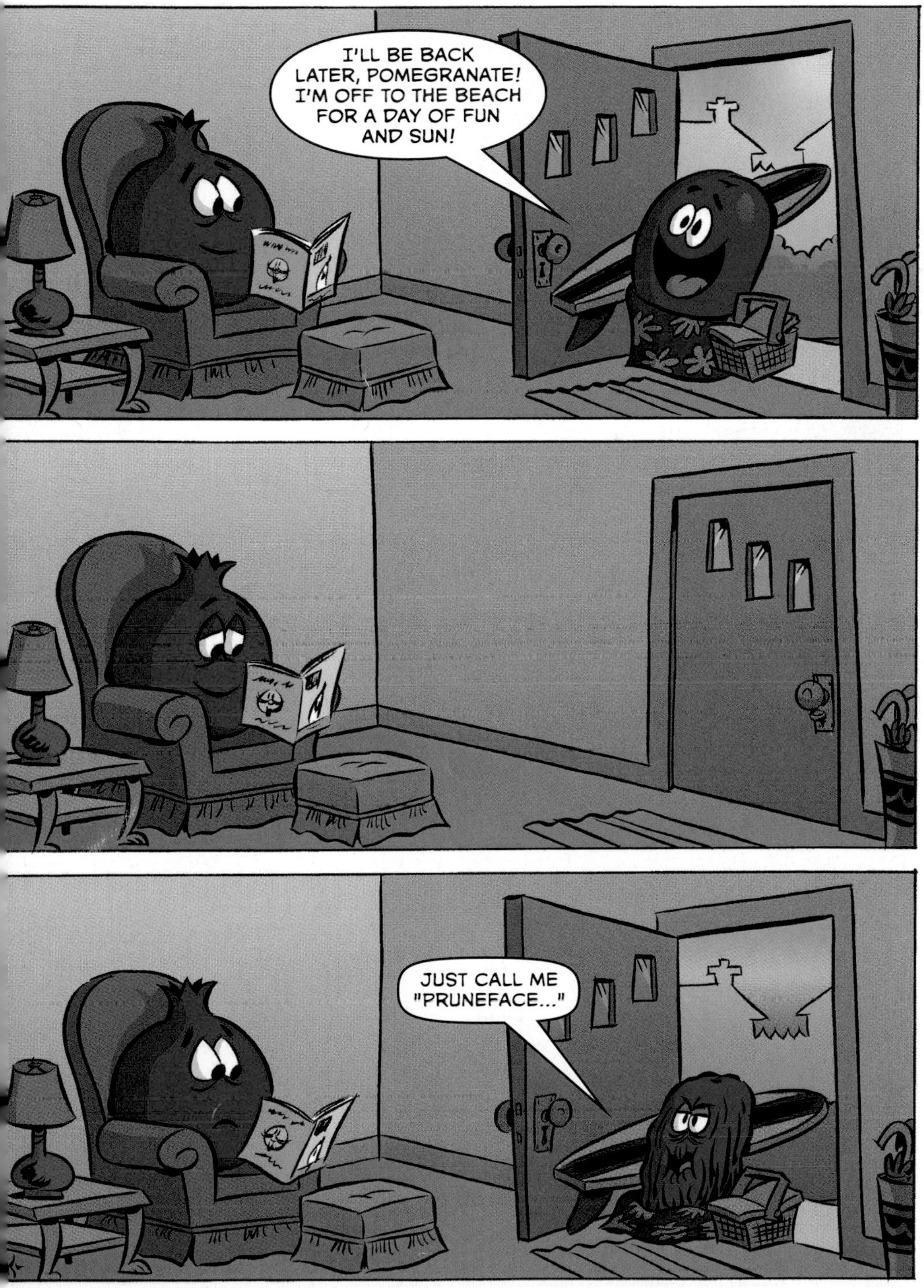
I'LL BE BACK LATER, POMEGRANATE! I'M OFF TO THE BEACH FOR A DAY OF FUN AND SUN!
JUST CALL ME "PRUNEFACE..."

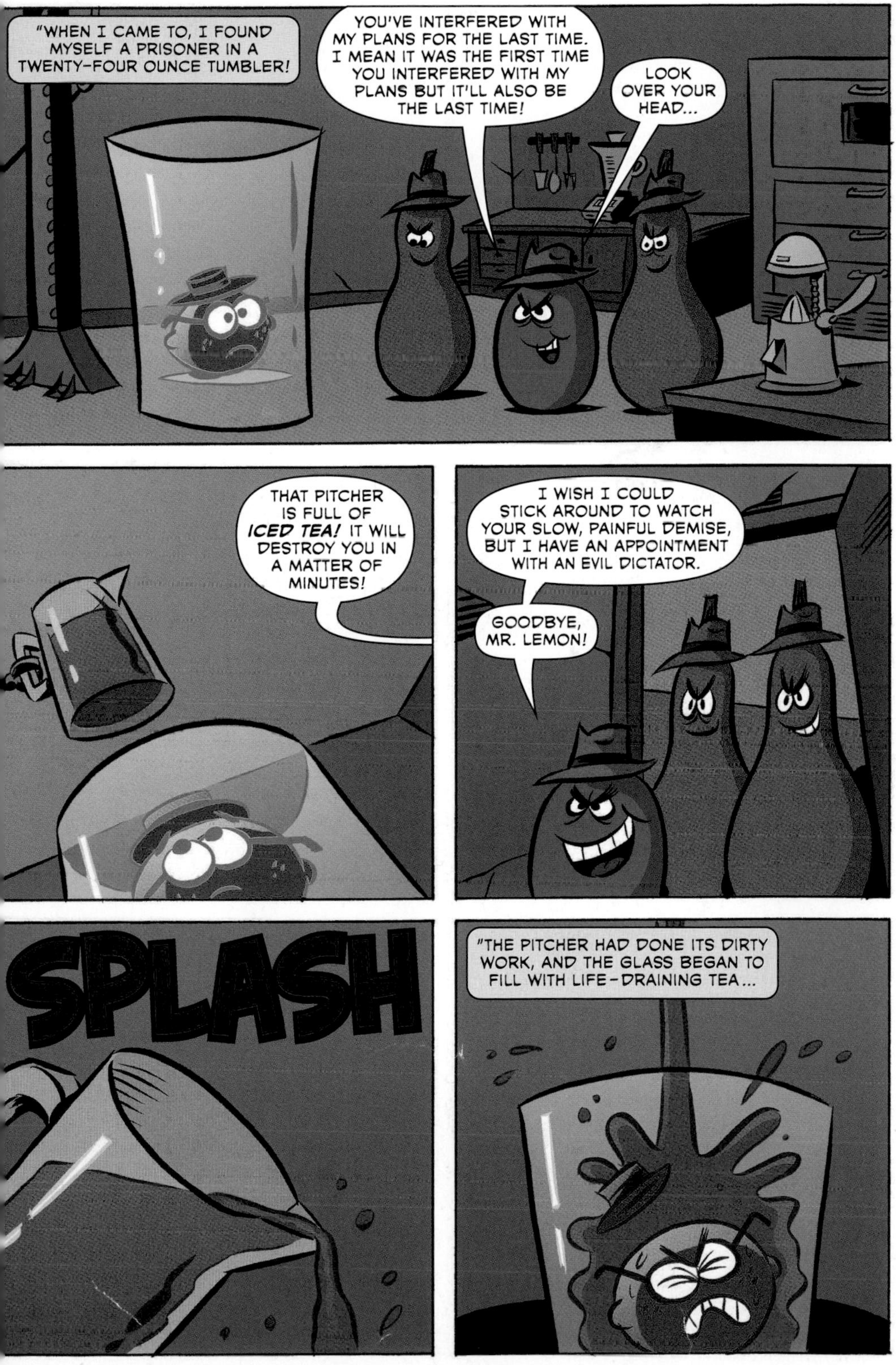
"WHEN I CAME TO, I FOUND MYSELF A PRISONER IN A TWENTY-FOUR OUNCE TUMBLER!
YOU'VE INTERFERED WITH MY PLANS FOR THE LAST TIME. I MEAN IT WAS THE FIRST TIME YOU INTERFERED WITH MY PLANS BUT IT'LL ALSO BE THE LAST TIME!
LOOK OVER YOUR HEAD...
THAT PITCHER IS FULL OF *ICED TEA!* IT WILL DESTROY YOU IN A MATTER OF MINUTES!
I WISH I COULD STICK AROUND TO WATCH YOUR SLOW, PAINFUL DEMISE, BUT I HAVE AN APPOINTMENT WITH AN EVIL DICTATOR.
GOODBYE, MR. LEMON!
SPLASH
"THE PITCHER HAD DONE ITS DIRTY WORK, AND THE GLASS BEGAN TO FILL WITH LIFE-DRAINING TEA...

A Bedtime Story

"ONCE UPON A TIME, LITTLE ORANGE RIDING HOOD WAS WALKING THROUGH THE WOODS. HE HAD GOTTEN A BIRTHDAY CARD FROM THE STATIONARY AISLE AND WAS ON HIS WAY TO GIVE IT TOO GRANDPA LEMON EVEN THOUGH HIS BIRTHDAY WAS TWO YEARS AGO.

"SUDDENLY, A BIG NASTY GRAPEFRUIT JUMPED OUT FROM BEHIND A TREE AND WITH A CRAFTY SMILE ASKED:

WHERE ARE YOU GOING ALONE IN THE WOODS AT THIS TIME OF DAY, LITTLE ORANGE RIDING HOOD?

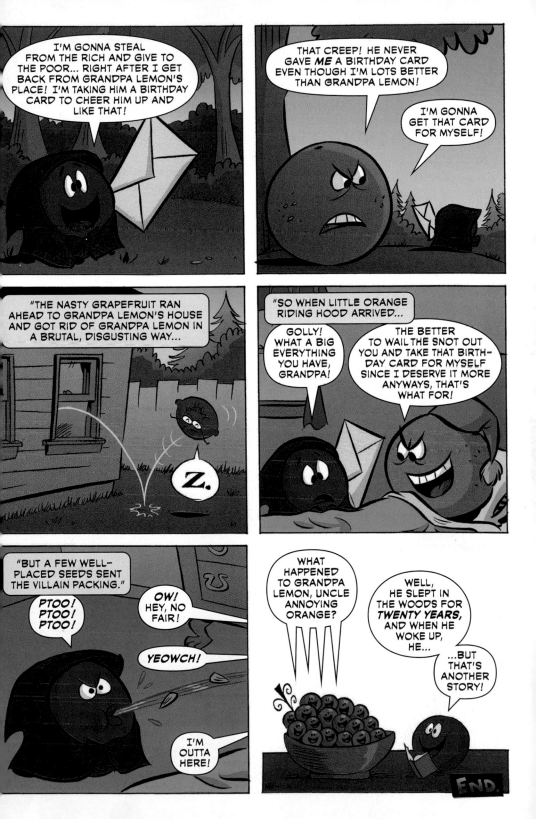

WATCH OUT FOR PAPERCUTZ™

Welcome to the fantastic, fruit-filled first ANNOYING ORANGE graphic novel from PAPERCUTZ. We're the folks dedicated to publishing great graphic novels for all ages. I'm your annoying Editor-in-Chief, Jim Salicrup, here to offer a little behind-the-scenes info on the making of this sure-to-be-a-valuable collectors' item graphic novel.

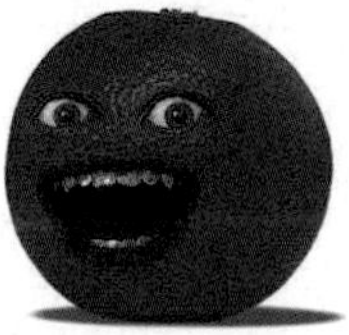

Of course, it all started with Dane Boedigheimer, the goofball filmmaker* who created the transmedia sensation known as ANNOYING ORANGE. Even though Daneboe brings forth new ANNOYING ORANGE videos on a fairly regular basis on YouTube, there is still a vast hunger for more Orange! Even with an all-new TV series on the CARTOON NETWORK, Orange fans remain unsatisfied. It is at this point, sensing the pent-up yearning for more ANNOYING ORANGE that Papercutz so unselfishly agreed to publish an all-new series of ANNOYING ORANGE graphic novels! Even though we're convinced that even this comicbook incarnation will only continue to create even more demand for more, more, and even MORE ANNOYING ORANGE! At this point it's merely a matter of time before you'll soon be bombarded with ANNOYING ORANGE: The Motion Picture, followed by the inevitable ANNOYING ORANGE: the Broadway Musical, and much, much more!

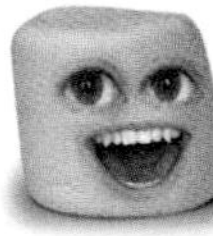

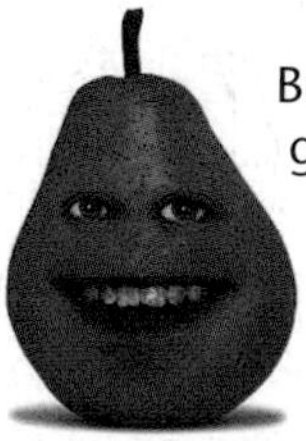

But until then we sincerely hope you'll enjoy the ANNOYING ORANGE graphic novel series! Created under Daneboe's ever-watchful two left eyes, and written and drawn by two contributing cartoonists to the TV series, Mike Kazaleh and Scott Shaw! (Yeah, the exclamation point is part of his name...), we're confident we can deliver that FRESH SQUEEZED COMEDY™ that you love so much!

In fact, to attempt to satisfy your curiosity concerning the mystery men responsible for all this, we present on the following pages, brief biographical essays on Daneboe, Scott, and Mike (Mystery women Laurie E. Smith and Jayjay Jackson will have to remain a mystery... for now). And like all things concerning ANNOYING ORANGE, I'm sure all this will simply leave you wanting more, more, and even MORE. So, just because we kinda like you, we'll be back in just a few short months with just that—more, more and even MORE with ANNOYING ORANGE #2 "Orange You Glad You're Not Me?" You're an apple if you miss it!

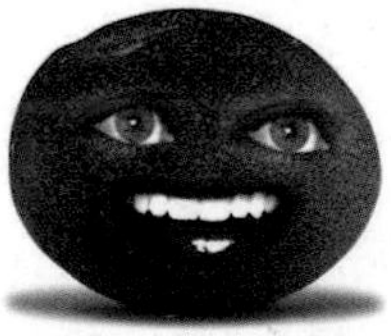

Jim

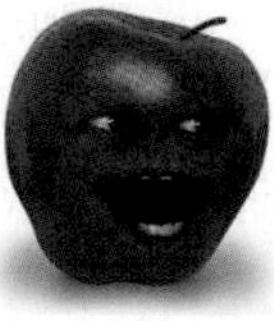

STAY IN TOUCH!

EMAIL:	papercutz@papercutz.com
WEB:	www.papercutz.com
TWITTER:	@papercutzgn
FACEBOOK:	PAPERCUTZGRAPHICNOVELS
REGULAR MAIL:	Papercutz, 160 Broadway, Suite 700, East Wing, New York, NY 10038

*Hey, that's what he calls himself! See for yourself on the very next page!

DANE BOEDIGHEIMER

Dane (or Daneboe as he's known online) is a filmmaker and goofball extraordinaire. Dane spent most of his life in the glamorous Midwest, Harwood, North Dakota, to be exact. With nothing better to do, (it was North Dakota) at around the age of twelve, Dane began making short movies and videos with his parents' camcorder. Since then he has made hundreds, if not thousands of short web videos... many of which are only funny to him. But Dane has remained determined to make "the perfect short comedy film;" one that will end all social problems and bring laughter to all the children of the world.

Currently, Dane is most widely known for creating  one of the most successful web series ever. Orange has over 2.4 million subscribers on You Tube, 10 million facebook fans, and has over 1.1 billion video views total. On top of that, the Annoying Orange series premiered on CARTOON NETWORK, boasting the #1 telecast of the day among boys 6-11 and has a complete line of toys, shirts, and other merchandise currently in JCPenney & ＲＵＳ amongst other major retailers.

Not to be completely undone, Dane's other videos have been viewed over 650 million times and have been featured on TV, as well as some of the most popular entertainment, news, and video sharing sites on the Internet.

In Dane's downtime he enjoys... oh, who are we kidding? Dane doesn't have any downtime. He wouldn't know what to do with himself if he did.

SPENCER GROVE

Spencer Grove has written plays, prose, television scripts and more online videos than any sane person should attempt. Also, he bakes a mean apple pie.

He began his career in independent productions, working on everything from infomercials to award shows, eventually moving to MTV where he served as an Associate Producer on Pimp My Ride. Since 2009, he has served as the head writer of the Annoying Orange web series, creating and co-creating the supporting cast and developing the ever-expanding online world of the Orange.

SCOTT SHAW!

Scott Shaw! is an example of Hunter S. Thompson's statement: "When the going gets weird, the weird turn pro." An award-winning cartoonist/writer of comicbooks, animation, advertising and toy design, Scott is also a historian of all forms of cartooning. After writing and drawing a number of underground "comix," Scott has worked on many mainstream comicbooks, including: SONIC THE HEDGEHOG (Archie); SIMPSONS COMICS, BART SIMPSON'S TREEHOUSE OF HORROR and RADIOACTIVE MAN (Bongo); WEIRD TALES OF THE RAMONES (Rhino); and his co-creation with Roy Thomas, CAPTAIN CARROT AND HIS AMAZING ZOO CREW! (DC). Scott has also worked on numerous animated cartoons, including: producing/directing of John Candy's Camp Candy (NBC/DIC/Saban) and Martin Short's The Completely Mental Misadventures of Ed Grimley (NBC/Hanna-Barbera Productions); Garfield and Friends (CBS/Film Roman); and the Emmy-winning Jim Henson's Muppet Babies (CBS/Marvel Productions).

Above an example of Scott's storyboards for the ANNOYING ORANGE TV series

As Senior Art Director for the Ogilvy & Mather advertising agency, Scott worked on dozens of commercials for Post Pebbles cereals with the Flintstones. He also designed a line of Hanna-Barbera action figures for McFarlane Toys. Scott was one of the comic fans who organized the first San Diego Comic-Con, where he has become known for performing his hilarious ODDBALL COMICS slide show. www.shawcartoons.com. Scott is also a gag man and storyboard cartoonist on Cartoon Network's ANNOYING ORANGE program. His favorite fruit is forbidden.

MIKE KAZALEH

Mike Kazaleh is a veteran of comicbooks and animated cartoons. He began his career producing low budget commercials and sales films out of his tiny studio in Detroit, Michigan. Mike soon moved to Los Angeles, California and since then he has worked for most of the major cartoon studios and comicbook companies.

He has worked with such characters as The Flintstones, The Simpsons, Mighty Mouse, Krypto the Superdog, Ren and Stimpy, Cow and Chicken, and Bugs Bunny, as well as creating his own independent comics including THE ADVENTURES OF CAPTAIN JACK. Before all this stuff happened, Mike was a TV repairman.

SOME EXCITING SCENES FROM OUR NEXT GRAPHIC NOVEL!

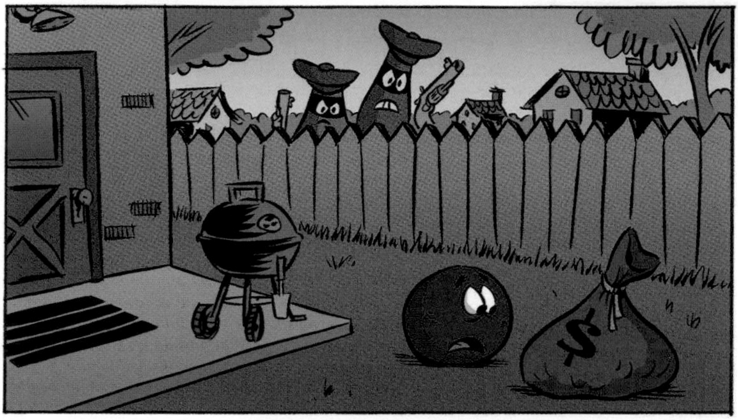

ORANGE, THE FAMOUS WORLD WAR I FLYING ACE GETS SHOT DOWN BEHIND ENEMY LINES. THERE HE FINDS THAT THE LUFTWAFFE HAS INVENTED A NEW SECRET DIRIGIBLE THAT COULD WIN THE WAR. CAN ORANGE DESTROY THE BLIMP AND GET BACK TO HIS OWN SQUADRON IN TIME?

THERE IS A DROUGHT ON THE ORANGE FARM AND THINGS LOOK DIRE. IF GLUEPOT, THE FAMILY HORSE CAN WIN THE PENNSYLTUCKY DERBY, THEY COULD USE THE PRIZE MONEY TO BUY IRRIGATION EQUIPMENT. UNFORTUNATELY THE EVIL COLONEL QUINCE HAS ENTERED HIS HORSE IN THE CONTEST, AND HE WANTS GLUEPOT TO FAIL SO HE CAN BUY THE ORANGE FARM FOR PENNIES ON THE DOLLAR.

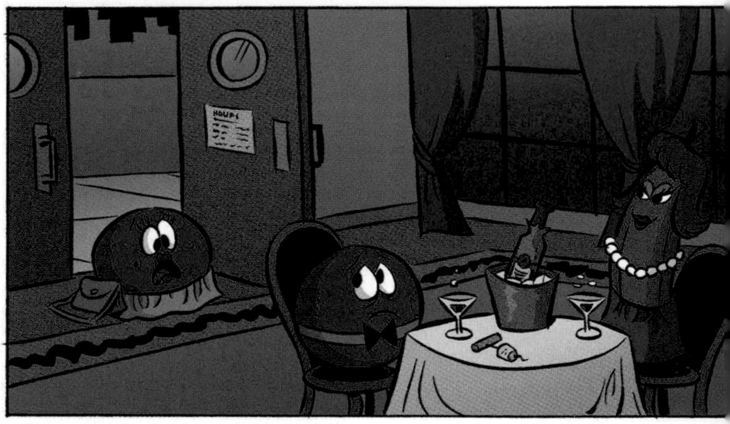

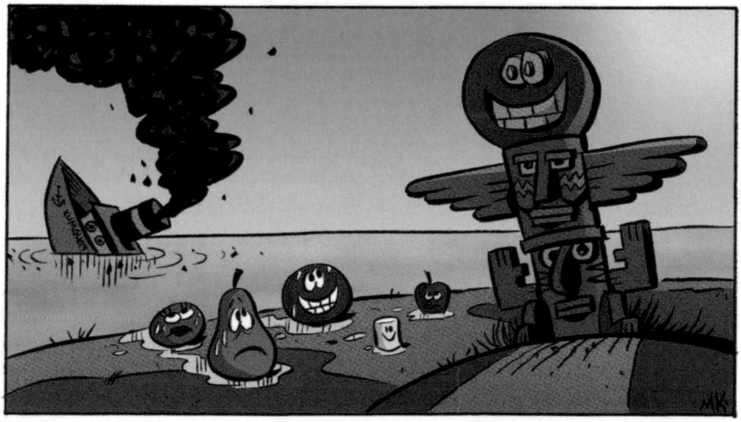

ASTRONAUT ORANGE ATTEMPTS TO BE THE FIRST FRUIT TO ORBIT THE PLANET JUPITER. THE FANTASTIC SPEED OF THE EXPERIMENTAL ROCKET HURLS HIM BACK IN TIME AND HE FINDS HIMSELF TRAPPED IN A WORLD OF PRIMORDIAL PRODUCE. THIS DISCOVERY WOULD BE A GREAT BOON TO SCIENCE IF ONLY ORANGE CAN SURVIVE AND RETURN TO HIS OWN TIME WHICH ISN'T ANY TOO LIKELY REALLY.

100%
Not from Concentrate

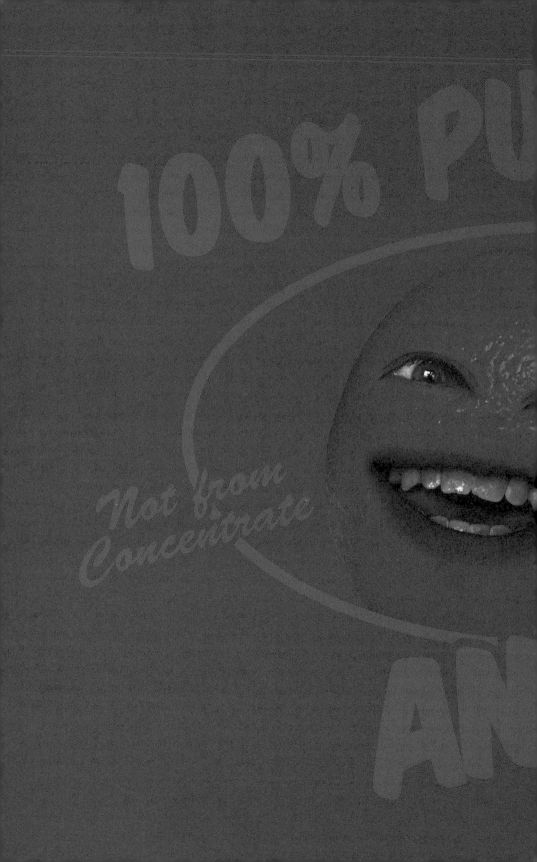